Beyond the Mirror:
Volume 2
Fantastic Worlds

BLAZE WARD

Knotted Road Press
www.KnottedRoadPress.com

**Beyond the Mirror: Volume 2
Fantastic Worlds**
*Copyright © 2014 Blaze Ward
All rights reserved.
Published 2014 by Knotted Road Press
www.KnottedRoadPress.com*

Blueberry was originally published as part of the novella *Rebels*, available from Knotted Road Press

ISBN: 978-0692237953

*Cover and interior design © 2014 Knotted Road Press
www.KnottedRoadPress.com*

Beyond the Mirror:

Volume 2
Fantastic Worlds

BLAZE WARD

Also By Blaze Ward

Beyond the Mirror: Volume 1 Fantastic Worlds

Stories
Approacheth the Wyvern
Rebels

Brak Stories
The Meat Shield
The Popcorn Kitten

Suren Stories
The Slave Market

Kaleph Stories
Death Key for the Great Khan

Poetry
The Desert Ring
The Forestal
The Mirror

Table of Contents

The Horse Thief	1
Lokisdotter	19
Blueberry	29
The Changestorm	39
Destiny	69
the Blacksmith's Song	87
Falling into the Dragon's Spine	103
Greater Than The Gods Intended	125

Forward

I went and looked back at *Fantastic Worlds, Volume 1* today, and am amazed at just how far Blaze has come in such a short amount of time. He continues to get his butt in a chair and write. He finishes what he writes, going through redrafting and editing stages. Sends it to his first readers, then listens to what we say, learns more, and produces even better final drafts.

A lot of writers talk about writing. Blaze committed to writing like a professional early on. People are amazed at his output. It's really a matter of building good habits.

Butt in chair. Fingers on keyboard. It's as simple, and as difficult, as that.

It helps that Blaze has a rich and varied history of characters that he's already familiar with for him to draw on. However, he also has a habit of finding these new people for you to get to know.

It's been wonderful going on this journey with Blaze, watching him grow into his storyteller role, getting to share these stories with others.

I hope you're enjoying this journey as much as I am.

Leah Cutter
July 2014

Introduction to Volume Two

When we first started talking about what would turn into Volume One, I had no idea how much fun it would be to finally commit to being a writer. All the ideas have been in my head for as long as I can remember, but now I can share them. And the responses I have gotten from readers have been wonderful, even if they generally complain that they want more of a particular character because I left the story without the Happily Ever After.

Those are rare, by the way. You have an adventure, and then move on and have the next one. Much of what is contained in here are the single adventures that combine to make a lifetime of fun.

Because this was always intended to be a collection of fantasy stories, it was Fantastic Worlds. But I also have plans for @lien Worlds, Heroic Worlds, Wild Steam Worlds, and so on. In the near future, I plan individual fantasy stories, like charms, until I can create enough material to create character-centered collections, which was always my goal. Hopefully, you will find characters you like enough to join me on that journey.

And none of this would be possible without a Most Wonderful Woman™. That you are holding this book reflects Leah's belief that I could do this thing, when even I had doubts. And it could not have been birthed without her hard work, along with my other First Reader™ Adrianne, and their commitment to Making Good Chairs™.

I can't ever say thank you enough to either of them, but I wanted you the reader to understand how much they have meant, even though you only see my name on the cover. It is always a team effort.

And readers are part of that team.

Thank you.

Blaze Ward
July 2014

The Sarmatian and his half-elf Sidekick return for more adventures, now traveling up-country to locate the Queen of the Night Elves as part of Suren's quest. I enjoyed this piece because it let me play with concepts of magic and history to explain how the world that might-have-been might have become the world that might be. Only fools fight in a burning house, but sometimes the issues become good and evil, rather than us and them.

The Horse Thief

Why do you even own a sheep?"

Suren the Sarmatian paused, coiled his long russet-coloured snake tail beneath him, shifted his weight back, looked up from his task to see Enica feeding the object of her query a fresh carrot.

For a Brigante forest barbarian and former slave of the Romans, the young half-elf woman with the scrunched-up face cleaned up well. She also continued her disguise as an adolescent human boy, dressed in a rough tunic, jacket, and leggings made by local tribespeople. Her strawberry-blond hair was pulled back, tied to keep it out of her face, with just enough left loose to cover her semi-pointed ears.

They had similar-enough features that he could tell people she was his "half-breed son," but for his chestnut hair and the fact that Suren's body consisted of three feet of elf atop nineteen feet of snake tail covered in tan and brownish scales. He was Sarmatian, after all, while she was just a half-elf.

Around her neck, the torq he had magically bound to her at the Roman slave market when he bought her. Karelian gold from the far northern steppes inset with a pair of hexagonal black onyx stones. Magically powerful materials. At her belt, the bronze knife he preferred, while in her hand the iron blade she used as a general tool. *Iron, fah.*

Suren carefully laid out the shirt of golden-coloured scale armour he had been attending, glanced at the night sky to estimate the hour, considered his...questioner? *Slave? Well, technically true, but rude. Assistant? Scout? Emissary?* She glared down at him. *Why did he own a sheep?* "As a reminder."

That made her delicate elven features scrunch up even more. Very confused. "Reminder? Of what?"

Suren sighed internally. *Another one of those conversations.* He gathered the clumsy Celtic words together in his mind. Latin lacked the subtlety, though Celtic was barely any better. Sarmatian had fifty-three different words for rain, most of them curses. "A reminder that this is a cold, wet, damp, rainy island."

She started to say something but he overrode her words. "That the only reason I'm not constantly miserable is wool harvested regularly from the noble sheep and transformed into the magically warm sweater I will continue to wear, at least for another three months." He plucked at one sleeve to emphasize the local wool covering his torso and arms, twitched the last meter or so of his tail a little closer to the fire to warm it. "Your people should worship sheep, not eat them. Cows are for eating."

Suren watched her blink to process that statement, open her mouth, close it again, think some more.

When several moments of silence passed, he stripped off the sweater in question, slipped into the scale mail tunic he had been oiling. Also Karelian gold, pressed into small sharks-tooth-shaped scales, glimmering in the firelight, brighter than the earth-coloured scales that covered him from mid-torso to the end of the blunt tail.

Suren shrugged to settle the armour, carefully laced it firmly into place. He reached under a nearby blanket and pulled out his crossed shoulder harness holding the Moonblades. He drew each blade, etched with their names, **Ucadan** and **Qürub**. **Waxing** and **Waning** for the crescent moons they resembled, and his favorite nights to skywatch.

A quick examination, and he slipped the harness around his shoulders, settled everything, put the warm, cream-coloured, British sweater back on. It was cold tonight. Probably would rain again as well. *Rain, fah.*

He watched her face, saw the curiosity at war with her natural reticence. And always sarcasm. "Are all Sarmatians like this?"

He grinned ever so slightly, expecting something much sharper. She had been born with a razor-sharp wit and a sarcastic tongue. "Perhaps. She has a name, you know."

"Who does?"

Suren pointed to their nearby companion, happily munching on a pile of fresh-cut clover. "Her."

"You named the sheep?" Sarcasm dripped like warm honey.

Suren smiled in spite of himself ."Indeed. Enica, may I introduce you to Argo. Argo, this is Enica."

Argo continued to munch, sheepishly oblivious to the diplomacy at hand.

"Argo? What kind of name is that?"

"It is Hellenic. From the ancestors of the people of Achaia." He watched confusion spread across her face.

Suren scowled to himself. He continued to confuse her without meaning to. "A Roman land far to the southeast. A land of warriors, scholars, and poets long before Rome ever came into being." Again, a blank look.

Suren oozed a little closer to the fire for warmth as he thought, re-coiled his tail beneath him, settled close to his half-elf companion. While her clothing made her look mostly-Roman, that was a thin layer over her Brigante wildness. He needed to remember that she really was a barbarian, underneath it all.

Strawberry-blond hair. Bright eyes, someplace between blue and green, followed his every move like a rabbit eyeing a hawk. Unfortunate, but necessary yet. At her belt, a Roman knife. Iron. Again unfortunate. Again, necessary. "Enica, this is important to me. Can you read?"

That same, guarded, look came into her eyes. A closed face. Silent. *Embarrassed?* Better to deflect this now, before insecurity took root. Suren reached for a nearby travel bag, opened it, withdrew a satchel wrapped in well-worn leather, handed it to her.

Good, honest confusion now, an improvement.

Enica sat gracefully, legs crossed under her to hold the package. She unwrapped it, looked inside. She reached in, pulled out a leather-bound book. "What is it?"

Suren reached out, carefully folded back the cover to reveal an inscription in a neat hand. "The object is a codex, made in the Roman style. A very significant improvement over the Aegyptian papyrus scroll. Contained inside are the writings of Apollonius of Rhodes, writing some four centuries ago. It is a long story poem called *The Argonautica*."

Suren watched her with some trepidation, weighing the value of the book and gaining some insight into her psyche against the concern that she might mistake the ancient tales for more of his *sorcery* and damage the codex.

Enica seemed to understand the great value of the artifact at an unconscious level, handling it with care. She cautiously turned to a random page, scrunched up her face at the rows of Greek symbols crawling across the page. "What is it?"

Suren nodded to himself, reached out a hand, touched a word on the page. "This is the word for Argo, which was the name of Iason's ship on his quest for the Golden Fleece, as well as my sheep. Would you like to learn to read? It will open up whole new worlds of knowledge for you. You might even appreciate the joke behind the names of the chariot ponies." He grinned broadly as she rolled her eyes at him.

"You named the horses as well?"

Staked across the clearing, Suren eyed two of the shortest, ugliest, dumbest horses he had ever encountered in his broad travels across Asia and Europa. *Just the way he liked them.* A local breed, native to the peninsula far to the southwest, near to Isca Dumnoniorium, utterly phlegmatic about pulling a chariot driven by a giant snake-man. Dumb, and calm. *Perfect.*

Suren uncoiled, slithered past her, approached the two hairy ponies. Behind him, Enica rose, followed. The nearer one, a chestnut mare, blinked at him, about as excited as she ever became.

Suren scratched her lightly under the chin, watched the ears happily flop in different directions. "This is Pholus. The other one is Chiron." The sable-colored colt whickered, nosed her pockets for the carrots he smelled.

Her face took on a slightly more mischievous glint. "More Achaian names?"

"Correct. Famous Centauri philosophers. Technically Macedonian, but I won't bore you with the difference."

He watched her sarcastic wit grow more bold with a sly smile. "I thought you didn't like horses. You curse them often enough."

"Ah. No. I don't like horsemen. Specifically Scythians. Specifically, barbarians from the northern steppes. Sarmatians do not move quickly on flat terrain. We can climb almost as fast as a spider or a squirrel, but even bow-legged tribesmen can outrun us. Thus we stay in the hills and canyons of Colchis and Alba. We have a special term for cavalry."

Enica patted Chiron on the neck, watched him graze stupidly. "The Roman term is *Equites*." He watched her spit angrily on the ground. A tail flipped, possibly in agreement. "Those were the bastards that ran us down and captured us at Lindum."

Suren waited a moment for the rage to step back from her eyes before he continued. "The Sarmatian term translates roughly into Celtic as '*fresh meat*,' and '*shit-head riding fresh meat*.'"

He watched her blink rapidly, processing.

He smiled. "Stupid barbarians do not like to walk. And much so cheaper for us to eat their horses instead of our cattle." He thought for a moment. "There are other interesting ideas contained in my books. I could also teach you to read the language of the Zhou from the distant lands of the east. One of their greatest generals wrote a very good book on tactics and warfare, ambush and misdirection." He smiled slyly, watched the idea take seed in her mind.

An evil smile joined it. "I would like that."

Suren nodded, pleased that he had made a breakthrough with this smart, half-elven girl. No. Woman. Enica was many decades older than she looked. Half-elf. Never forget that. And this way, perhaps, she could preserve the words of her people, lest they disappear. He knew she was dismayed at how quickly her people were adapting to the Roman way.

Suren slithered back over towards the fire, found a smooth flat spot in the dirt to work. "This is the first letter in the ancient Achaian tongue. It is called *Alpha*."

Enica came awake suddenly with a desperately bad hangover, a dry tongue, the taste of a three-days-dead mollusk in her mouth. The southeastern sky was just beginning to pale with the promise of a coming dawn. A few clouds scudded across the constellations, lonely and forlorn. She took in the camp with a glance, saw the fire nearly dead, the contents of her bags scattered nearby.

She groaned, sat upright, groaned again, focused through the pain stabbing behind her eyes. "Suren." Damn. She could barely hear herself speak. She swallowed over the dry tongue, swallowed again, fought to her knees. "Suren." Good. Louder that time.

Overhead, the leaves rattled as branches moved. A head appeared upside down from the tree, concern for her written across his elven features. "Enica, are you well?"

His words broke the spell over her limbs. She staggered to her feet, drew her little iron knife, looked around the campsite. Good, her bow was still there. What happened?

"We appear to have been subject to the depredations of a thief." Was he answering her? Had she spoken aloud? Maybe. Maybe he was just thinking the same things she was.

"Why does my head hurt so much?"

She watched his concern turn to...something. Anger? Slowly, the rest of him slithered out of the tree, coiled beside her. A whispered word drifted across the campsite, followed by a flash of soft light. For the briefest moment, everything seemed bathed in bright purple ink.

She watched his torso rotate in place to look in all directions. It was like watching an owl when he did that. His scowl could break rocks. He approached her carefully.

"Here. Stand very still. Please." A naked hand reached out. She had rarely seen him without the heavy gloves he habitually wore. He had oddly delicate hands for the amount of strength in them. He touched her forehead. Bright blue sunshine. Morning. Butterflies. Normal. What had happened?

"We have a horse thief on our hands." The voice of doom. DOOM. A very angry Sarmatian. A look that might curdle stone.

"Enica." Blink. What? Was he speaking to her?

"ENICA." Yes, definitely speaking to her. The hand withdrew. Fingers snapped in front of her. CRACK. Flash of light.

"What?"

He relaxed a shade as she spoke.

She took a deep breath, felt spring invade her bones, drive out the winter resident. "Ow."

His scowl turned into a wry grin. "Our horse thief is also a hedge wizard. This presents a problem."

She watched his hands clench and relax, clench and relax. *Am I drunk?*

"No, not drunk. Overloaded with eldritch power this morning. Perhaps drunk. A form of drunk."

Oh, shit. I'm talking out loud. Stop that. Deep breath. Release. Control.

"So what's th' problem?" *Good, that sounded almost normal.*

She watched his fists clench and relax, as if grasping a throat. "I despise thieves, even horse thieves. Normally I would hunt him down and feed him to the worms in pieces. That would be such a waste here."

Okay, he wanted another response. Deep breath. "Waste?" *Rational. Almost back to normal. Breathe again. Maybe sarcasm soon.*

He scowled fiercely. "There are very few with the talent for sorcery in this world. To destroy one, especially in light of what is coming, would be a crime against everything I am trying to prevent."

Had she ever seen anyone that angry before? Yes. Once. Uncle Tanti. Yup. Bad things gonna happen.

"You don't even like horses."

"He took Argo."

Dead man.

❧

Suren circled the camp a second time. Inside the path he cut, he heard Enica add a few branches, built up the fire. Not that either of them needed it. There was enough moon out tonight to read any trail.

He glared at the ground again. Glowered magnificently.

Normally, there would be enough moon. Not enough this morning. Little sorceries.

This horse thief was a hedge wizard. Just a little sorcerer. But enough to bury the tracks of himself, two horses, and that stupid sheep. Himself? Yes. The traces had a masculine flavour to them. Faint. But distinct. *Himself.*

Suren broke his circling, returned to the spot next to the fire. He could sense Enica's face pale a bit when he drew both of the Moonblades, examined them carefully, drive them point down into the dirt, close at hand.

He opened his pack, pulled out a hollowed cow's horn. Opening it, he sniffed carefully, dipped in, pulled out a pinch of deep green powder. "It was fortunate I prefer to sleep in trees. And that he was in a hurry."

Beside him, he felt her shift, unconsciously knowing what was coming next. "Why is that?"

"He might have taken my casting materials and made it very difficult to find him. Plus I have all the silver." He glowered, breathed once, tossed the pinch into the fire.

Suren muttered his incantation in a language even older than Sarmatian. He concentrated on a specific rune he had learned and pushed. The universe pushed back, intent on thwarting his will. He growled at it mentally, surged, felt the barrier fail. The night seemed to turn inside out for the briefest heartbeat.

Beyond his flesh, the fire swallowed itself for several seconds, turned emerald, blinked back into existence. He heard her hiss of surprize. "What the hell is that?" He opened suddenly closed eyes, exhaled slowly. Smiled. Unknotted the kinks in his tail.

A difficult conjuring, but a rewarding one.

On a warm rock squatted the creature. Technically, it had a dozen limbs, not eight. Eight eyes, though. Hungry eyes. Angry eyes. Lethal ones. Red. Golden fur covered the cat-sized body. Acid dripped, almost oozed, from the mandibles. "That is a fire spider."

He sensed her recoil, her confusion, her surprise. He sighed, but only inside. "That's a fire spider? Then what did you show me in the slave market before you rescued me? Bought me. A demonic shrew?" She must be feeling better. The sarcasm was back in her voice.

Suren turned to face her, deadly serious graven on his face. "What I showed you at the slave market was an illusion. A cheap and easy sorcery, designed to impress upon you the seriousness of my quest."

"You lied to me."

"You are human. Such lies do not count."

She started to rise, taking his bait. "Half human."

He smiled, cold, grim. "Human enough." Pointed at the thing before she could speak. "That is a fire spider. Once summoned, it must take a life, a *human* life, before it can be unthreaded. Would you have been willing to be that human?"

She blinked, processed, sat back down. "So you're going to kill him when you find him, even though he's a sorcerer?"

"We shall see, Enica. We shall see."

Enica ghosted softly through the morning underbrush, her plum-coloured flatbow strung. Ready. *It still needed a name.* Before her, the fire spider skittered slowly through the needles and fallen limbs of an old forest. She shivered, in spite of herself.

It wasn't as bad if Enica thought of the creature as a particularly quiet hunting dog. Except that it...*drooled?* Did spiders slobber with anticipation? Dogs did, but dogs didn't slobber acid. She passed another spot, smoking slightly. Barely the size of the nail on her little finger, but the tang had a bite even several steps removed. Nasty. Harsh. *Death.*

Enica could see the tracks now. Apparently the sorcery their hedge wizard had used was only effective for a few hundred yards. Now they were in open forest. Her territory. A twig bent here. A leaf torn. The slightest mar of a hoofprint, not quite brushed over by a fresh-cut branch. Yes, this hedge wizard, this horse thief, was very good. Almost as good as her. *Almost.*

Her family used to call her a wild shadow, accused her of talking to trees and rabbits. Close enough. Nobody had ever been able to track in the deep forests like her. If not for...No. Don't think that. Roman cavalry. Roman soldiers. Rome. Chains. Slavers. Vengeance. Later.

Enica dipped her chin. Just enough to bring her jawbone into contact with the golden torq bound to her neck by the Sarmatian's magic. Enough magic to track her. She didn't doubt that now. Enough for a fire spider to find her. But enough to buy her out of a Roman brothel, or a tin mine, or an early grave. And a promise of freedom. Soon. Finish the quest. Send the Sarmatian home. Then kill Romans. All of them.

Something in the flavour of the forest changed. Enica noticed it before the fire spider did. Stopped. Dropped to her haunches with the flatbow in front of her, nocked. Prepared. Tasted the air. She felt/saw the spider stop, turn to look back at her. She shook her head at it, unsure how intelligent it was. Dogs couldn't walk sideways like that. Nor keep one eye on her and the others forward. But it paused. Squatted down. Watched her.

Behind her, the wind. Except not the wind. Keelscales oozing quietly over bark, leaves, mulch. Suren slithering close. *How could something/someone so big move so quietly?*

She turned a glance back as his smell reached her. Masculine. Elven. Something else. Sarmatian? "We're very close. He dens nearby."

Suren studied her face closely, nodded silently to himself, reached up both hands to touch the pommels of the Moonblades at his shoulders, stretched. A torso of elf atop four and a half yards of snake. Earthquakes rippled down the tail and back.

Enica shook her head as she watched him, broke her reverie. She sniffed. "Smoke. Breakfast. Lucky for him." She smiled grimly at her companion.

"How so?" Suren coiled into a tight bundle, able to leap any direction.

"He's cooking bacon, not sheep."

"Yes. Indeed lucky. Perhaps. Where?" The immense scowl lessened, promised only eternal damnation.

Enica pivoted her head, back and forth. Her right hand stretched out, pointed. "There. One hundred yards, perhaps one hundred fifty." The forest around them was solid, undulating over hills and the occasional brook. Impassible.

She watched him transform back into something dark and malevolent. "You approach directly. Quietly. He will not be expecting you, but will be prepared. Perhaps a warding. Perhaps a guard animal. Possibly both."

"And you?"

"I will surprise him." The scowl could have carved stone.

⌇

Enica waited, breathed, became one with the trees and brush around her. Disappeared. Ahead of her, a foe as dangerous as a wounded boar.

Suren's fire spider had left with him, leaving her alone in the trees. As was proper. Five paces. Pause. Smell. Listen. Absorb. Know.

Bacon. Much fainter now. Perhaps eggs fried in bacon grease as well. Faint. Done cooking and eating now. No dogs visible, but eggs meant chickens, or possibly geese. Noisy when surprised. But stupid. Be invisible to them. Again pause. Circle in place. Check for a dog moving laterally, thinking to hunt her. Check the arrow. Nocked. Sharp. Deadly. Another five paces. Pause. There.

A clearing. Perhaps twelve paces across. Nine wide. Artesian well feeding a pool and a small stream. A doorway set into the hillside. Closed. Fresh dung. Horses. Sheep. Argo. Chiron. Pholus. She waited. Absorbed the texture of the place. Reached out a hand, started to stand.

"If you value your life, you will not move, boy."

The tongue was Celtic, not Roman. Something cold touched the back of Enica's neck. Sharp. Insistent. She froze. Something clawed at the edge of her mind. Black. Hostile. Bad. *Sorcery.*

The voice was male. Older. Perhaps old. Rusty from disuse. Angry. Smelled garlicy. The man smelled badly too. Unclean. How had he snuck up on her? *Nobody was that good. Were they?*

"Drop the bow carefully, or I'll gig you like a frog." The point of the knife prodded again. Just enough to threaten, but not quite break the skin. "Now, boy."

Enica released the arrow, let it fall, sent the bow after it very carefully. She took a deep breath. Contained her anger. Remembered Suren. And a fire spider. *Good luck, horse thief.*

She felt the man pull her iron knife, take it from her. A rough hand shoved her into the clearing. Followed. The horses whickered. Argo munched. The hand spun her around.

Human. Male. Old. Leathery. Dirty. Angry. *Good.* Angry people make mistakes. He pointed a thing at her. It looked like a square iron rod, heated and twisted into a coil. Maybe meant to look like a unicorn's horn. There were still a few in the deeper stands of the wild country up north. But ugly, wrought, iron. Rusting, too. Suren would be extra angry for that. He truly hated iron.

The human raged without speaking, apparently gathering the words and remembering how to fit them together. "How did you find me?"

She considered his anger. Poked. "Tracked you. T'weren't hard. Your forest craft is fading, old man." Goad him. Make him angrier. Rely on the Sarmatian. *Rely?* Shit. Yes, rely. Let the sorcerers fight it out. And the fire spider. Always the fire spider. Ugly, golden-haired devil hound.

"Impossible. You're no wizard. Just a forest-boy. I could have killed you last night. Tell me why I don't kill you right now and take everything from you?"

Suren's voice had an angry, rumbling timbre to it. Like an avalanche of hungry demons baying down a hillside. He must really like that sheep. "Because you would like to live through this day."

This was going to be fun to watch.

The human spun, confronted the Sarmatian coiled between him and the door to his hut. Backed a step to keep Enica in front of him. Stood at one point of a triangle, suddenly at bay. Nervous rage.

"What in the deathlands are you? Some sort of snake-demon?" The point of the iron spike stayed centered on Enica. She thought about moving, paused, poised, just in case. That thing looked nasty.

Enica heard all sound from Suren stop, a sure sign he was coiled up like a spring and poised to to make one of those amazing leaps that no human could duplicate. She didn't dare turn to look, in case the spike suddenly moved.

Suren's voice could have grated stone. Maybe they did worship sheep where he came from. "I am a Sarmatian, human. The horses and the sheep are mine."

"And the boy?"

"Mine as well. I am willing to gather my things and depart in peace. You are a wizard. I would choose not to destroy you, this morning, given the option. There are few enough of us left in the world."

Enica watched the rage in the human's eyes detach from her, drift across the clearing to Suren. It was like watching fog move in a soft breeze. Something else left with it. There was less weight on her back, on her mind. *Damned sorcerers.*

The human's voice turned very strange. Hoarse. Raspier. Deeper. "I will destroy you, snake-man. Snake-demon." The iron spike moved, pointed at Suren now. No knife. Well, the little bronze one, but nothing useful to kill a man. She needed a sword. A club. Something. Perhaps just an opportune distraction. Wait. Listen. Strike. *Buy a sword next town. Absolutely.*

"Truly, that you can use an iron athame to work your sorceries impresses me. But iron limits the power. If you used bronze, or aurichalcum, you might be one of the most powerful of us." Suren's voice had a hypnotic quality. Enica blinked hard against the seductive tones. *Deep breath. Focus.*

The human seemed to grow more angry with each breath. *Another sorcery?* Calm her. Agitate him? Angry people make mistakes. Mean bastard. Sneaky, too.

The human raged. "Bronze is for elves and the other dying races. Iron is the power of the future."

Suren's tone changed. Barely controlled anger added a sneering layer of salt to the words. "Iron is the tool of engineers. Of Romans. It will destroy all the magic in this world and leave you alone and powerless. Do not make me destroy you."

The human scoffed, a mad light in his eyes. "Your gold athame cannot stop me, even if they do look like swords. I will destroy you now, monster." Enica heard him mutter something that transformed into a scream as it came out of his mouth. A bolt of...*something* coalesced on the spike, leapt across the space at the Sarmatian almost faster than the eye could follow.

Suren stood firm, leaned back as if facing a stiff wind, the Moonblades crossed before him where the spines bent forward. *Were they glowing?*

The bolt of power impacted on the blades, splashed. *Splashed?* The glade grew bright and hazy. A strange green fog seemed to seep out of the water and ground.

Enica thought to move, but was rooted to the spot. Watched a drop of sweat fall from the human, hang halfway in the air. Had time stopped? *Sorcery. Maybe.*

Suren grunted through pain and effort. "Human. This can still end well for you. Surrender and I will spare you."

The horse thief's eyes grew large, unfocused. "Die, die, die, die, die." The words had a strange, unhuman cadence, the mind behind them suddenly unhinged. Enica pushed against walls of honey encasing her mind, failed.

She watched the human's rage suddenly shift back to her, center. *Uh oh.*

The spike looked like the prow of a ship pointed at her chest, seemed to swell to the size of a mountain. Something black and malevolent plucked at her soul with greedy fingers, cold pain. Her heart forgot to beat. Death-scent in her mind. Black wings swelling around her, encompassing her, tugging at her. Brass horns played.

Pain.
Darkness.
Night.
Emptiness.
Weightless.
Light.
Dawn.
Sunlight.
Day.

"What have you done?" The human's screaming, anguished words gave form to her existence again.

Forest glade. Brook. Chicken shit. Horses. Argo. Morning. Horse thief. Suren. *Blink.*

Suren hung over the human, rage quivering clear to the tip of his tail. Moonblades in each hand. Glowing? Smoking? Something. The human down to one knee. His right hand was, gone? No. Shriveled. Blackened. A little knot of death at the end of his arm.

The iron spike, the *athame*, lay sundered at the human's feet. Two pieces of twisted black iron, red hot, smoldering the leaves. *Dead unicorn.*

Suren raged down with a glare sufficient to curdle milk. "I have broken you, human. Iron blocks the magic. Bronze channels it. As does Karelian Gold. Do you wish death?"

Enica shook herself like a wet dog. Her brain began to slowly reassemble itself from razor-sharp shards. Smoke assaulted her nostrils, grounded her reality. *Power.*

The hedge wizard began a chant, piercingly high. The notes scratched the insides of her mind like claws. Reality unraveled again.

"ENOUGH!" Suren's rage broke through the fog in Enica's mind. She grasped it like a drowning sailor might hold a floating spar, held it to her soul. She felt whimpers seep out of her chest.

And then a star exploded.

It might have been mere moments later. Possibly days. Enica's skin felt crisp and tight, like a sunburn. Her eyes remembered how to open, focus. The image would haunt the rest of her days. As would the screams.

The Horse Thief. The Hedge Wizard. Face down in the mud. Screaming. Thrashing. Dying. Fire spider on his back, biting. Blackness consuming his skin like wet wood, but from the inside. Liquid red glow breaking through, oozing like blood. Burning blood. Acrid, acidic smoke.

Rabbits died like that. But quieter. Much quieter. Audible for only miles. Not lifetimes.

Finally, death.

Enica took a painfully deep breath, pulled life back into her lungs, exhaled smoke and death. Stood, after only three tries. Wobbled.

Suren reached out a hand, braced her until the world stopped spinning. Provided a solid spot. Earth. Mountain. Sarmatian.

"What was that?" She was proud her voice sounded almost normal.

Suren turned that gaze on her, softened it to just rage. *Just? Just.*

"That was death magic. The most powerful kind of sorcery. The most dangerous."

"What happened?"

She watched him consider several answers before he spoke. "Iron and magic are incompatible. When I broke his athame, the power backlashed into him. And broke his mind. So he tried to cast the same spell without an athame. It might have killed us all. But I brought a fire spider."

Enica glanced down at the human's body, saw only a pile of human-shaped ash smoldering like charcoal. Smelled fresh coal and pork. Considered puking. Contained it. For now.

The fire spider caught her eye, blinked all eight of his. No. Hers. She clashed her mandibles together with a faint click. Smiled? Faded out of sight.

Enica shivered. "Yes. A fire spider."

She looked at her feet, bent, picked up the two shards of iron, still warm through her leather gloves. "Was he more powerful than you, Suren?"

She heard him take a deep breath, hold it, release it. "Much. But also completely insane. And evil. Perhaps even a necromancer." She watched the blunt tail reach out, stir the collapsing pile of ashes, mix them with air and soil and leaves and water. His voice quieted, as if talking to himself now. "Better he be destroyed. There will be others I can teach."

Enica breathed. Just that. Walked over to the horses, scratched Pholus under the chin.

Breathe.

Many of the characters I write about evolve out of my gaming experiences, being characters I have run as a player, or created as a GM, or just thought about but never gotten around to. Alicia d'Aubert was one of those. I have created and run her in three different gaming engines over the last couple of decades, changing her each time. For this story, I wanted to go back to her origins (as I had written them up in the most recent campaign) and bring her forward to the point where her adult campaign started, when she was already well-rounded and distinct. Here, she is a teenager poised on the brink of adulthood, confronted by something at once grand and terrifying. How would you react to being a pawn of the gods themselves?

Lokisdotter

C'mon, Alicia."

"I don't want to."

"Well I don't want to get in trouble with your mother."

"We're not kids any more, Ealisaid. Are you afraid of her?"

Ealisaid looked around Alicia's semi-frilly bedroom, took a deep breath and gave her friend the most-serious, grown-up look the teenage demi-orque could manage. "No."

Alicia looked up from the gold wires she was carefully weaving into a necklace, floating magically in the air before her, and tried to return the serious look. It dissolved into giggles instead. "Are, too."

Ealisaid smacked her friend on the shoulder. "Am not."

"Are, too."

Ealisaid put on a regal air, straightened her back for a little extra height, and attempted to look down her nose at her best friend in a dignified manner. "Fine," she huffed. Being half a head shorter than Alicia put her at a significant disadvantage.

Alicia gave her friend a sidelong glance. "Fine, huh?" She relaxed her eldritch grip on the piece and let it settle slowly into her lap.

"You're not going to be the one that gets a good talking to, little miss mint," Ealisaid grumbled.

"Oh, so Ealisaid is afraid of her, after all." Alicia grinned.

Ealisaid got a gleam in her eye. "Am, not." She quickly gestured with one hand, muttered a glyph, pointed at Alicia's right foot, and turned her left sock lime green.

"Hey," Alicia exclaimed, "you cheated."

"Did not."

"Did too."

"Maybe you should tell your mom so you can get me in trouble."

Ealisaid watched her friend stop, concentrate her focus for a moment, and transform both of her socks a deep, rich indigo. Then she added a thicker layer of wool to the outside to make them warm, while she was at it.

Alicia stuck her tongue out. "That was six years ago, Ealisaid. It's what nine-year-olds do. We're supposed to be adults now. Have to act like it." She huffed once and flipped her long, magenta, ponytail for good measure. The firelight made her facial tattoos stands out bold and fierce.

Ealisaid grinned. "Maybe," she said, "but you have to practice. If you aren't going to, I'm supposed to be studying." She gestured again, turned Alicia's pink shirt orange.

Alicia glanced down, gave her friend a sour look. Without a word, she breathed once and shifted the color to a pure white linen. "Studying, huh? You could always go bother, Illiam. I'm sure he'd be happy to see you."

Ealisaid suddenly perked up. "Do you know something?"

Alicia grinned. "Maybe. But I'll only tell you if you promise to stop bothering me."

Ealisaid grinned slyly. "Oh? Am I bothering you, missie?" She gestured again, added yellow polka-dots to Alicia's formerly blue sweater.

"Hey. Cut it out."

"It's called practice," Ealisaid said. "I'm supposed to work my great and mighty, awe-inspiring, dread eldritch skills at you. You're supposed to stop me. You're the big, bad enchanter chick, you know."

Alicia turned her sweater crimson. "Don't you have any other tricks?"

Ealisaid glowered. "Look, fashion magic is about the best I can do. Not all of us are powerful sorcerers who can make diamonds from coal, you know." Alicia's leggings developed off-square stripes.

"Stop it."

"Make me."

Ealisaid raised her hand and began to point. She heard Alicia's voice as if from a great distance. "I said stop it!" And then she blacked out.

The voice sounded terribly familiar. "Ealisaid? Please wake up. I'm sorry."

Ealisaid considered the warm darkness, decided her butt was cold, opened her eyes. "Huh?" Alicia hovered over her, concern written on her beautiful demi-orque features. "Gods, I am so sorry. Are you all right?"

Alicia helped her sit upright. Ealisaid found herself on the floor next to the bed with a sore butt and a knot on the back of her head. She rubbed it absently. "Ow. How'd I get here?"

Ealisaid felt Alicia move around behind her, fingers moving carefully through the long, raven tresses until she encountered the growing goose egg on the back of Ealisaid's skull. Coolness suddenly flowed into the knot, relaxing it. Warmly goodness flowed through the rest of Ealisaid's body.

She sighed.

Alicia moved around in front of her and took her jaw in one hand, turning it one way and then the other. "Let me see."

Ealisaid gazed at her through a mild, friendly fog. "See what?"

Alicia touched the center of her forehead with one long, elegant green finger. "Whoops. Here."

Ealisaid felt the fog dissipate with a pop. Alicia helped her to her feet.

"Oh. What happened?" Ealisaid said quietly as she looked around.

The room looked like it had been looted by a troop of drunken gnomes. Cups and trays were scattered even more haphazardly than normal. A tapestry hung askew from one wall. The vase of dried meadow-flowers had been knocked over, scattering petals onto the floor. Alicia's necklace project was a small coin-sized puddle of gold on the quilt instead of a beautiful lacing of fine wires.

"Uhm," Alicia began, "I kinda overreacted. And bounced you off the bed. Sorry."

Ealisaid blinked and stretched her jaw, but nothing hurt. "Ya know, maybe I should leave you alone to study. I can go bother Illiam or something."

"Oh, no," Alicia said, grabbing her by the hand before she could take a step. "You're staying here and helping me clean up."

"Why me?"

"Because you started it." Alicia gave her a wicked grin.

"Oh, no you don't, little miss mint," Ealisaid replied. She gestured around the room. "I was doing fashion magic. About all I can do, I'll remind you. This was all you."

"I wouldn't have done this if you weren't bothering me. Your fault."

"Is not."

"Is too."

The door to Alicia's bedroom flew open suddenly and banged into the wall with a thump that made both girls jump.

Alicia's mother, Arielle, seemed to flow into the room, legs moving so smoothly under her gown that she looked like a jade statue on wheels. Even though she was a full orque, she was extremely beautiful. She glanced around the room with a critical eye, speared the two demi-orque girls with a moue.

Both girls squirmed in the extended silence.

Alicia looked at her mother earnestly. "So. You, uhm, heard that?"

Arielle's mien turned very serious. "I felt it, Alicia. The entire village felt it."

Alicia stared hard at the floor. "Sorry, mother," she mumbled.

Ealisaid mirrored her best friend's pose. "It was my fault, Abbess."

Arielle raised an exquisite eyebrow at both girls. "I doubt that. I suspect two highly-strung teenage girls were acting like teenage girls. Please clean it all up and keep yourselves in better control. We will talk more at dinner."

Both faces turned the color of burnt umber as red blush flooded light green skin. Both girls kept their eyes on the floor until they heard Arielle depart. The door slammed handlessly, just as it opened.

Alicia glanced up at Ealisaid with a grin. "Is too."

⌒⌒

Alicia lay bundled against the mid-winter cold as the fire settled down. The moon hung low on the eastern horizon, leaking light

22

slightly through the shutters. The keep was settled down and quiet. Bakers were a few hours from firing up their great ovens. Guards marched in the square outside. She awoke from a doze to uncertain sounds.

"*Alicia.*"

She wasn't sure if the sound was real or a dream. Blue eyes opened the faintest slit, registered the whole of the room from tucked in deep under quilts and furs. Something about the fire caught her eye. A face floated in the flames.

"*Alicia.*"

She wove a barrier around herself and then sat up, in the order her mother had repeatedly pounded in to her head over the years. She was finally listening. The gold bracers Arielle had insisted she wear at all times lit up, the twin burgundy disks on them faintly aglow with her magic.

"Who are you?"

The flaming eyes focused on her, bored into her soul for a second. A small bit of flame detached itself and floated into the center of the room. As she watched, it slowly expanded and transformed into the shape of a man.

Alicia climbed from the bed and prepared a number of spells. She held off crying for help, for now. The room was well protected by her mother's magics, as well as her own, so the visitor must be very powerful. Or extremely sneaky.

He completed his transformation and smiled at her. He even bowed sweepingly, a sardonic smile on his gorgeously-human features. "Greetings. I am a messenger."

Alicia wove another spell across the space between them. She felt very grown up. She wasn't screaming or blasting things with spectral bolts, not even once. She even half-curtsied. "Good evening. A messenger from whom?"

Just in case, she wove a Knowing and sent it floating across the room at him, but it bounced lightly off him like a wave striking a seawall.

Alicia considered the man who stood before her. He appeared human, but was extremely tall and well built, towering half a head over Alicia's six and a half feet. She was tall for a demi-orque, and had heard stories of humans that were taller than her, but never met one.

He was beautiful in a masculine way, rather than ruggedly handsome, and wore very fine silks and cloths. She appreciated the craft it took to clothe him, especially after so much practice with Ealisaid. Long brown hair hung down and partially obscured the bright blue eyes that smiled at her. They studied each other for a long moment more.

"Why, from the Great Trickster himself," the stranger said. He wove a hand and a complex rune hung maroon in the air between them, the sign of the sect Alicia's mother headed.

The Cult of Loki.

Alicia caught her breath.

Before she could respond, however, the door to her room flew open and her mother entered. She moved much less elegantly this time.

Arielle carried a strange-looking shortspear in her hands, with a silvered boarspear tip and a perfect emerald the size of her thumbnail set at the exact center of the crossguard. The emerald glowed almost as fiercely as Arielle's eyes in the dim light.

The stranger turned as Arielle entered. He smiled warmly at her. "Hello, my love."

Arielle stopped as if she had walked into a wall, shock written on his features. "You."

The man bowed. "Indeed."

Alicia stood perfectly still and watched the byplay between the two, uncertain of the tides of energy and emotion playing out unspoken.

The intense glow in Arielle's eyes and in the spear's emerald both faded slowly as she unraveled her spells. "Surely there's more time?"

The man's smile transformed into something more grim. He turned to face Alicia, and studied her carefully. "She has come into her power. There is nothing more you can teach her at this point."

Arielle's shoulders slumped in defeat. "She is my daughter. It is my way to shield her, to see her raised well."

Alicia felt strange to be discussed in such a detached manner, as if she were a fly on a wall. The emotions flowing about the room tasted strange to her magically-enhanced senses, all grown-up and subtle and knotted. She watched, silent, uncertain.

The stranger walked carefully around Alicia, never closer than arm's reach. She could smell the rich scent of pines and spring flowers about him, even as winter held sway outside.

He stopped directly in front of her, facing her from four feet away. There was a smile in his eyes to go with the one on his face. "And you have succeeded, Arielle. She is strong, and quick, and beautiful. But she cannot stay here any longer. *They* will know where to find her now." He turned back to face Alicia's mother, grim determination written hard in his bones.

Arielle nodded to herself. She sat the shortspear down on the buttcap and let it take some of her weight. "Could we not all flee again?"

The man shook his head. Alicia was astonished to watch her normally-dominant mother, the powerful Abbess of the Cult, look so soft and plaintive. His voice, however, cuddled her close. "No, my love. She must find her own way now. You must flee, but it will be to draw them after you instead so they will miss her tracks. And then her quest can begin."

Arielle stumbled to the bed and sat heavily. Alicia sat beside her to put an arm around her mother. Arielle held her in turn. "So soon." She kissed her daughter on the forehead.

Alicia looked first at her mother, and then the stranger. "My quest?"

The man's smile turned to hoarfrost. "Many centuries ago, the elves arrived in these lands and warred with the orques who lived here. Your ancestors. To win the war, and block the future, they located the gate to the middle lands and sealed it from this side. The All-Father, the Thunderer, the Gatekeeper, the Word of Law. All were all trapped on the other side. It took me centuries to find a way through the bars, tiny as a flee, through a stitch they had missed. You must find the anchor that is the key to the spell and unravel it."

Alicia sat patiently and thought for a moment. "Why me?"

The man drew himself up to his great regal height. "Because the elves wove it such that no mere mortal could overcome the magic, while blocking every one of the Gods."

Alicia blinked in confusion. "Mere mortal? What does that make me?" She felt Arielle's strong arms clasp more tightly around her, but her mother remained silent.

The man looked over her one more time, an examination almost clinical. "Potentially, a new god."

Alicia felt a shock roll through her frame, starting with a cold pit of fear in her belly. "How?" was all she could manage to get out.

The man nodded. "Because you are my daughter."

Alicia looked coldly at the man. She could feel an icy rage surge up, begin to take hold of her. "And just who do you think you are?"

The man bowed formally, one hand sweeping the floor as though at court. He smiled sardonically at her again. "Ah, of course," he said. "You did not know. I am the son of Fárbauti, the father of Hel and Vánagandr. I am Loki, commonly called The Deceiver."

Alicia felt the bottom drop out of her world.

This story was kind of an accident. I had just finished the piece that would become Lokisdotter in this volume, and I was all set to continue the introduction into a much larger piece detailing the beginning of Alicia's quest. However, when I got my butt in the chair, I felt this (metaphorical) tap on the shoulder, followed by "I dinna think so, lad."

Cullen and Shrike didn't let go of me until I completed the whole tale, of which Blueberry is the first piece. The whole, Rebels, is available from Knotted Road Press, and represents my first novella in a very, very long time. I plan to return to Utanum.

Blueberry

Lad, do I even dare t' ken what yer up't' nae?"

The new-comer's voice was gruff and deep, gravel grinding between millstones. Its owner, another orque, had the grizzled, frayed-edges look of hard decades of harsh sun and frozen winds to his greenish orque-skin as he stood in the doorway.

Shrike glanced up from his workbench, giving his visitor a put-upon look. The small cast-iron cooking stove in his tiny shed provided very little light to work with, especially with the open door blocked by a body. He needed sunlight. He would have growled at anyone else in the village, but the visitor was Cullen.

Gnarled green hands, strong, picked up an arrow from a wooden shelf nearby, lifted to sight it with a critical eye, noting four fingers of stained discoloration along the back of the shaft where the arrow would be fletched later. The middle-aged orque sniffed hesitantly. "Cherry?"

Shrike blinked in surprise that older orque recognized the flavor. The other orques in the village tended to be opposed to any sort of new idea that might permeate someone's thick skull and make things easier. The elders of the tribe, Joruhn in particular, were a big enough pain already. He wasn't in the mood to listen to old Cullen wax philosophical about the so-much-superior ways of his grandsire and how soft kids were these days.

Not today.

Shrike stayed where he was, squatting by the small iron pot and stirring the softly boiling liquid over the low flame with a stick. He gave a grunt, sufficient enough for a reply.

Cullen replaced the first arrow, carefully lining it up with the rest of the batch, then moved to a second group, already dry on a lower shelf. He grabbed another arrowshaft. This one showed several inches of a much lighter brownish stain to the light-colored wood. A pink tongue snuck out, sampled the wood, withdrew. "Peach?"

Shrike nodded once, went back to his pot. The liquid bubbling within was a soft green.

Cullen stepped close, took a sniff over Shrike's shoulder. "That's pear," he said. "Can't imagine yer makin' a beer wit' it. What strange and wondrous idea have ye stolen from the pansies this time?"

Shrike looked up sourly. "No elf would ever get caught dead doing this. Nor any 'proper' orque." He went back to stirring. He liked Cullen, but wasn't in the mood to get into a scholarly discussion of orquish culture and tribal history this morning. He could always punch the older orque, he supposed.

Cullen sighed and sat on a nearby bench. "Dinna get me wrong, lad. Ol' Cullen's jes confused, is all. As is usual wit' you." He pulled a wineskin from over his shoulder and took a sip.

Shrike picked up a sheaf of fresh arrow shafts wrapped in a leather cord and pulled the first one loose. Carefully, he dipped one a hand's-width into the liquid and held it there for six heartbeats. He looked up at Cullen as he counted. "Move your ass."

"Why?"

"Because these go there to dry, you old coot." Shrike handed him the first shaft and pulled the second from the stack.

Cullen stood and carefully placed the wet shaft on the bench. He smiled with merriment. "How kin I help you, Shrike me lad?"

Shrike thought for a moment. He nodded at the cherry flavored arrows. "Javelin arrowheads are on the shelf. Long-distance, cherry-flavored, flight arrows. Go ahead and start mounting them to the dark-red shafts. We'll do fletching tomorrow." The second shaft was ready. The third went into the pear-juice.

Cullen grabbed a handful of light, sharply-pointed tips and a shaped-stone bottle of glue. "You do plan explain it at some point, right, lad?"

Shrike grinned at Cullen. "Not if you won't shut up, old man."

Cullen grinned back.

"It will probably only work in total darkness, Cullen. Bottom of a well at midnight dark. And it was the only way I could think of, to identify each arrow by taste or smell without taking my hand off the bow to check the tip, or wasting precious moments if I need to load for a second shot on the fly. Changing the fletching for each type of arrow was an idea, but that would change the flight characteristics too much. This way will work. I just need your help."

Shrike finished his explanation and rocked back onto his heels as he squatted next to the little cast-iron grill where Cullen cooked blood sausages for his dinner. Shrike listened to the late afternoon fall sounds as the birds settled around the village clearing. Stillness hung in the air over the sizzling of the grease and the fading of the afternoon light. Shrike kept his face composed.

Cullen concentrated on his wursts for longer than necessary before he pulled them off with an iron fork and set them on a wooden trencher to cool. He looked sidelong at Shrike for a moment. "Total darkness, lad?"

Shrike nodded with a serious look. Inside, he smiled. Joruhn would have stomped off by now. This was headway. "Absolute."

Cullen shook his head. "That, m'boy, has got t'be the third dumbest thing I've e'er'eard."

Shrike bit back his first sarcastic comment. Barely. Progress. "Third?"

Cullen shook his head. "You've met m'cousin, Gondrokeen, lad."

Shrike smiled slyly at the older orque. "And he's topped that? Twice?"

Cullen took a bite of his sausage, letting the warm grease run down his chin. "And survived both, too," he said. "What makes y'ken yull walk away from this?"

Shrike narrowed his eyes and grinned at his old comrade. "I'm willing to bet your life on it, Cullen."

"Ach, well. Dinna that just make it all dandy, lad?" Cullen said. "No."

Shrike smiled broadly inside. By this point in the conversation, not having been punched in the snout by Cullen was already a major win. Outwardly, he glowered sourly at the older orque. "It's an elf. They're rich. Filthy, stinking rich."

Cullen chewed industriously, like a goat on a particularly-fresh rose bush. "Oh, sure. Frilly little silk vests and cute leather leggings, probably kelly green like in all da fairie tales. I'd look right silly dressed that. Maybe a darlin' little rapier I could pick me teef wit', too?"

Shrike reached out hesitantly, then grabbed a sausage when Cullen didn't spear his hand with his fork. You never knew. "I'll give you his coin purse and jewelry free and clear. Anything that looks really good or maybe magical, we'll take to the Kolodny Brothers, sell it to them, and split even."

Cullen spit harshly. "Fah. Gnome pimps."

Shrike smiled and took a bite of blood sausage. "Maybe. But you're like to have gold in your hands this time."

Greed set its sharp little hooks in the older orque and tugged. Still, he wavered. "Unhatched chicks, lad."

Shrike considered the older orque's face for a moment. Time to get serious. "If you get dead, I'll hunt for your kin all winter and keep them in elk and riverfish until spring thaw. If the elf's got no gold, I'll bring you a whole buck for your trouble. With a little gold, you could buy enough flour to get the whole clan through the winter. Or hire a stoneshaper up from the coasties to build that little stone longhouse Britha keeps on you about."

Cullen shook his head. "Tis a swamp, lad. That be a right lot 'mount o'gold to raise stone. An' ya still haven't answered the important question."

Shrike narrowed his eyes. "What?"

Cullen gave him back a smile made hard by decades of swamp living. "Why?"

Shrike speared him with a sudden, hot look. He gestured east. "We live in a swamp, Cullen. Those lands used to be our forest, Cullen. Before the elves. Our people were here first. I get tired of those high-and-mighty Sylvan Lord elves coming here and invading our land and killing people," he snarled quietly. "And not just orques, but all the green folks. Two moons ago, they burned one of the goblin villages on the northern bluffs. Just walked in and set the buildings on fire."

Cullen nodded sagely. "I meant, what set you off, today, Shrike? Those pansies a'been here fer a long time. Why this? Why today?"

Shrike grimaced "Listening to your niece, Eatha, yesterday, talk about her constant nightmares, how she can't go visit your cousins on the coast for fear of an elven hunting party in the woods. And then I watch the elven villages push us farther and farther into the swamp. Eventually, we'll have to cross the Inner Sea or be wiped out. That's not right. I'll do whatever it takes. If I have to kill all the elves, I will."

Cullen sat quietly, intently, for a moment as he finished his sausage. "Aye, laddie. I know ye will. And I'll be wit' you."

Cullen stretched out on the grassy bank of a slow, broad river with his hat pulled down low over his eyes and his legs crossed, basking in the warm noontime sun like a lazy lizard. A cane fishing pole stuck out of the ground beside him an' trailed a length of string out to a bright-yellow float drifting idly in the current. A rope tied a stake beside him to a wicker weir trap down in the water, already occupied by the first two stupid-hungry trout to come along this morning. He took a sip of well-watered wine from his favorite skin and wiggled his butt back and forth a little to find just the right spot in the grass, then leaned back against a tree that had just the right width and slant and scratchy bark.

The forest sounds died off suddenly around Cullen. Hoofbeats cantered down the road across the river, coming closer.

'ere we go.

Cullen cracked open one eye to merely a slit to watch the lone rider across the water. He wasn't much in favor of horse, but that beast looked like it would roast down nicely on a spit, kinda like an ugly goat. Beautiful roan hair that looked to be curried daily by some prissy little groom. The kind of gloss to the coat that only comes with eating enough of the freshest oats and rye hay daily to feed three families o' his kin folk. One fancy iron shoe struck a chunk of flint and threw a flash of sparks as the creature approached the ford and began to swim majestically across.

On its back, Cullen watched the big poofing nancy boy spur it to greatest effort. *Oh, my. Gold spurs, m'lord? What a lovely sword you have, too. All the better to stick me with? And what fine chain mail. Did it come silvered or did your servants polish it up special this morning for you? And did you realize that it took an entire cow to get enough leather for all that saddle and tack, you rich bastard?*

The voice booming across the water could have been a pleasant and melodious soprano. On someone nicer. Instead, it was angry and harsh.

"You. Peasant," the rider called as she approached, her horse dripping water from the ford. "What do you think you are doing, poaching fish from my river?"

Cullen blinked. *Huh, a she-elf. As if anyone could tell, lookin' at 'em.*

The rider's personal gear was a bit of glorious elven poetry set to cloth, from the rich white-silk shirt under the low-cut chain armor showing her small cleavage and belly button to best advantage, to the fine, green-leather leggings laced to show a flash of perfect milk-white thigh, to matching knee-high riding boots with ornate silver buckles. She even wore a lovely silver helmet with a hooked nasal and wings coming out from the ears.

Cullen tried not to giggle at the image of a giant silver seagull perched on her shoulders. *Elves was always so full of themselves.* He stood up slowly as the rider came closer. He was unarmed and wearing simple forest leathers, so the rider came within thirty yards, safe in her well-made chain mail and carrying three feet of bare steel with a beautifully wrought gold pommel wrapped around an onyx stone.

Ya know, that sword prolly cost more than me da' earned in 'is whole lifetime.

Cullen scratched his ass with one hand and leaned back against the tree. "Yer river, lass?"

The rider halted her proud stallion and glared at him across the grassy gap. The horse snorted arrogantly at him.

"Indeed, it is my river, trespasser. I am the Baroness Renalon. I own this entire river valley, from Caleah all the way to Lafeld and the entire delta as well. What are you doing on my land, orque scum?"

Cullen picked his nose, examined the results, and rubbed it on his vest. *Damned elves always sounded like they was on a stage, or being followed around by a mincing little bard recording everyt'in' fer posterity.* "Fishing fer me dinner. The wee ones is hungry. Dunno anything about this being anybody's river. Them's me fish."

Lady Renalon climbed down off her horse with the grace of true elven nobility.

Cullen sneered to himself as he watched. *Bet she even sleeps at attention.*

She tossed her glorious blond waist-long braid to one side and pulled a well-polished kite shield from the horse's side. All the pretty pictures painted on the shield probably meant something really important, at least to someone who cared.

The she-elf strapped her shield on and slowly advanced towards him menacingly with her sword up. "No orques are allowed on my land, green scum. Time for you to die."

Cullen watched her advance slowly and finally lost his temper. "We was here first, ya poxie dandelion-eater."

She snarled inside her great silvered seagull head. "And we were born to rule you, peasant. Ileberat, Great Mother of the Elves, put your kind here for us, just for that purpose. I've killed your parents, your grand-parents, and their grand-parents. No orque will be allowed to survive. You are all just prey."

Lady Renalon swung her sword at Cullen.

Cullen easily danced back behind his tree to duck the blow, then snarled at the Baroness. "Yer almost right, ya daft cow. Not prey, though. Bait."

Baroness Renalon furrowed her flawless elven brow in confusion and paused her advance. "Bait?"

Cullen only heard the bowstring twang because the entire universe seemed to have stopped around him. Absently, he noticed a fish strike his hook and draw the yellow floater under the surface of the river. He hopped backwards before the dumb elf-lady could regroup her thoughts and run him through with that lovely silvered-steel blade.

Eight inches of barbed steel erupted from between those perfect elven breasts and transfixed her heart with a nice, meaty thump. The scent of copper from fresh-slaughtered pork suddenly filled the clearing.

The light faded out of Baroness Renalon's brilliant blue eyes as she died on her feet. She collapsed face down in front of Cullen, twenty inches of arrow shaft marking her demise, straight up in the air, quivering.

"Yup. Bait, ya blueberry-flavored racist," Cullen muttered with a sniff.

Across the stream, Shrike emerged from a covered blind they had spent yesterday erecting between the roots of two mangrove trees. He clutched the heavy composite reflex bow named *Redcaster* in one hand. Without pause, he nocked an arrow with a nasty-looking crescent shape and fired it into the horse's flank, then two more with regular triangular hunting tips as the monster turned and prepared to defend his rider.

Cullen ducked behind the tree again before he got kicked in the face.

After the second arrow, the stupid horse finally collapsed and Shrike began to trot to the ford. Cullen pulled the shield from the Baroness's arm and inspected it. "Ya took yer sweet time, ya bastard," he yelled. "Those two liked to killed me a'fore you gots involved."

It was a nice shield. Might be big enough for his daughter, at least until she got older. The sword went into a gorgeously tooled leather scabbard wrapped in gold wire and set with precious stones. Cullen sneered at how many tons of flour and barley this one poxie bitch wore as ornamentation while he and his stole through the swamp one step ahead of gators and really nasty critters, struggling to eat enough to survive. He kicked her corpse once for good measure, then realized what a dumb idea that was as his soft leather boots connected with a dagger hilt.

Cullen hopped like a graceful stork as Shrike arrived. "Not a word," he warned.

Shrike smirked. "Never crossed my mind, old man," he said. "Enough gold to make you happy?"

Cullen gave his friend a very serious look as he settled on two feet again. "Lad, they's'nough gold here t'feed the whole damned county fer two, maybe three winters. More if that sword's as magical as it feels and those boots are what I think they are. Why they gotta be like that, Shrike? Why?"

Shrike shook his head. "Some people think they were born better than everyone else, Cullen, so it gives them the right to take whatever they want."

Cullen shrugged and pulled a skinning knife from his belt. "Waste not, want not. I got the horse. What do we do with her?"

Shrike set his bow down, flipped the elf's corpse sideways, and began pulling his blueberry-flavored razor-leaf arrow the rest of the way through. "We'll take her gear and her armour, then I'm going to bury her under a cairn right here. The Kolodny Brothers will give us a lot of gold for all this stuff. And, one of these days, I'll tell Duke Henurdiy where to find her and they can take her home for a proper burial."

Cullen looked up from where he kneeled next to the dead equine beast. "Not going to make her long pork, me'boy?"

Shrike fixed him with a very hard look. "We're not savages, Cullen. Just taking back what's ours."

Cullen smiled grimly and began to cut. "Oh, I know, lad. Jest wanted to make sure you did. We've jest started down a very hard road, m'boy. Is gonna get wee messy afore we're done."

Shrike shrugged. "I didn't start this war, Cullen. They can go back where they came from any time they want."

The Changestorm

11th Day of Mahr: Beqdash

I ought to know better than to complain to the Gods. About anything. Seriously. It's gotten me in enough trouble already, and I'm not even that old. Yet. Of course, if I keep doing stupid things like that, I might not get there. And I'm not ready to leave a beautiful corpse. At least, not mine. Some other moron, fine, but leave me out of it.

Not that anyone would mistake me for beautiful. Cunning, perhaps. Tall, maybe. Half-drunk and performing birthday party illusions on the bar this afternoon, absolutely. Keeps the kids entertained. The locals, too, but they're grown-ups and not nearly as much fun. At least they pretend not to be, but I can see it in their eyes. And the Capering Camel occasionally needs to be reminded that the house wizard, such as I apparently turned into, also has a fun side.

The kids' mother, Aga, was down at the end of the bar keeping watch and tending as I made eight-inch-tall ogres and trolls sing and dance a squeaky chorus line across the old, stained wood. Emel, Aga and Serkan's youngest daughter, giggled and cheered like only a six-year-old can. Eser and Deniz, the only son and the middle daughter, tried to maintain a cooler composure.

At least until one of the trolls walked over and mooned them. Works every time.

Even Yagmur, the oldest daughter, had a smile for me today. But she's fourteen now and turning into a young woman. Way too serious. Rather pretty too, but none of the locals was going to do anything stupid in here, between me doing sorcery at the bar and Mother Gül at the other end of the bar knitting, with a heavy stick in easy reach.

And, of course, The Dog, curled up at my feet, watching everything that moved with a predator's eye.

I like to tell people I won her in a poker game.

True enough, if you allow for them playing with sharp iron sticks and me playing with eldritch energy and nobody using cards.

Did a little divination on her after I got her. Turned out her sire really was a wild Corsac Fox and her dam was a bull mastiff that belonged to a clan of Şimallı tribal warriors up in the Empty Quarter. Which made it pretty damned impressive, for a lone fox to sneak into a barbarian camp and get all the male dogs to chase him into the desert just long enough to get to the female coming into heat. And she got her daddy's brains. Interesting mix, too. Golden-brown eyes, long snout, kinda floppy ears. Mom's size. Dad's coloring and big, fluffy tail. A little magic, and she's adopted me. And the kids in the bar. Good momma dog, all around. Reasonable judge of character, in spite of liking me, but everyone's got their blind spots.

I felt the woman coming up behind me without looking around. The dog gave her a couple of friendly tail flips instead of a growl, so I didn't need to interrupt the puppet show just yet. I watched out of the corner of my eye as she walked around to the dog's side, crouched down, presented a fist for sniffing, gave the dog a couple of scratches behind the ear, and pulled up a stool.

"Does he have a name?" she asked. Young voice. Female. Clear. Bright. Cheery. Out of place in here, but it's Beqdash. Nobody actually belongs here.

"She," I replied, not looking up from the troll chorus line high-kicking on the bar. The tricky bit was coming up.

"She?" Bit of confusion. Not used to being wrong. Or being contradicted.

Wonderful.

Another Young Noblewoman. Welcome to the dirty part of town, lady.

"The dog," I said. "Haven't asked her. Feel free to."

And now the ogre synchronized finale. Ta-da. Giggling children and even a few adults. A couple of copper garsh tossed into a nearby mug, and, from the sound of it, a silver dinar. My lucky day. Not what I had planned, but I won't argue with it. Got happy kids. The rest was frosting.

"You haven't named the dog?" Oh, yeah. She was still here.

Not bad looking. Tall and kinda skinny. Very well dressed. Expensive tastes. Long brown hair up in some elaborate braid. Pretty blue eyes. Looks younger than Yagmur but isn't. Yagmur was just never that innocent.

Quick glance around the room. Party of outsiders over in the corner paying close attention to me and the girl. Weird bunch. Mix of genders and races you didn't see around here. Couple of elves, couple of humans, none of them couples. An agama. A half-orq girl giving me the evilest stinkeye, so this one must belong to them. Even a three foot tall Kipchak warrior that drank from a pint-sized mug. And the girl. All wide-eyed and important. Obviously never learned to play poker.

"Nope," I countered finally. "Assumed she had a name. She's never told me. You know how some women can be."

Ah. Now that's the kind of look I expected in a joint like this. Cold. Intellectual. Disdainful. Honest. The only grown-up females around here that would be happy to see me are the ladies of the night a couple of blocks over. And then only if I had enough coin.

I tented my hands and gave her my most innocent smile. I still needed to practice that occasionally. She hadn't huffed off yet, so apparently I still had some way to go before I got on her nerves. Be interesting to see where that line ended up being. Someday.

"You are," she said, working her way up to a good, cold, disdainful huff after all, "the wizard, Kaleph Sa'id, I presume?"

I smiled. "Presumably."

She glared for a moment. "I find it odd that you have not named the dog."

"It's a complicated story, m'lady. We're at a bit of loose ends, but I tell you what. You hire me for some big important job that pays a lot of money and I'll let you name her." I smiled my most oily smarm at her.

"Oh," she brightened suddenly. "That's why I'm here. To hire you, that is."

Use brain, then open mouth. I never got that sequence right. Crap. Couple of serious killers in that bunch over there. Smiled at me all friendly-like now. That just made it worse. This couldn't be good. On the other hand, I did have an honest Divination that said I'd be leaving town soon. At least before those Şimallı tribesmen came looking for their now-squished friends and their dog. And, come to think of it, why did this group need a wizard?

"And just why would you be needing the services of a wizard?" Innocent and ignorant was going to have to be how I played this. The publican, Serkan, Aga's husband, appeared with a bottle of Ubakh white wine and poured her and me each a glass. Without asking. So, she already had a tab going. And money. That stuff was spendy.

She took the glass and had a polite sip without looking. Definitely noblewoman material. High end. Loaded. Invincible. Welcome to Beqdash, Princess.

I guessed she intended to bat her eyelashes as me. Or had developed a nervous twitch. Not unique in the women who hang around me long enough.

"We are," she said importantly, "exploring in the Empty Quarter and found ourselves in need of the services of a powerful sorcerer. You come highly recommended."

I did? Who the hell knew me well enough in this town to recommend me? The Bey wouldn't, unless he wanted me out of town. And I couldn't imagine that he was still that mad. That left Zaztrol the Hyrcanian. I supposed this mob would have encountered the money-changer as soon as they landed and he did owe me a few favors. Including his mortal coil.

"And just what happened to your previous wizard?" I was playing a long-shot. They pay off occasionally. Her face dropped. Hell, her whole head dropped. Was she crying? Sniffling, in any case. Crap.

That brought the half-orq out of her chair and two steps in my direction, hands reaching for the broad-sword she had hidden under a cloak until just now, and a very cross look on her otherwise pretty face.

Oh my. This was going to get stupid ugly, quick. My house, my rules, little orq lady. I smiled at her, all friendly-like, and wound up a particularly nasty spell thread I kept handy for encounters with angry strangers in bars. It'd already been one of those weeks.

Her mistress saved her life. Probably thought she was saving mine. "It's okay, Hillevi." She took a sniff and waved the half-orq lady-in-waiting/ass-kicker/chaperone back to her seat.

I unwound the nasty little enchantment I had in my head. A little. Enough for now.

Princess took another sniff, pulled herself together. "You couldn't know, of course."

I nodded obliviously, tracked the half-orq back until her butt settled in the chair. "Of course."

"He was like a favorite uncle." She sniffed again. I suppose I was supposed to hand her a kerchief or something. She looked like she was used to having people like that around. "It was all such a terrible tragedy."

Half-orq babe, Hillevi, finally settled, grabbed a mug of beer, glowered at me. The dog settled back down too, her butt on my foot, her ruff mostly back down flat. "So," I circled back conversationally, "what happened to him?"

"He drowned."

He WHAT? This is the desert, lady. How do you drown in the desert? Get so drunk you fall off the end of the pier? Hell, even that hadn't killed me.

I picked up my glass, raised it to her in utter solemnity. "My condolences." Damn. That was good wine. I needed to meet more people like this. I couldn't afford it on my own. I could normally barely afford rent on my flop these days. Which brought me back to… "You said you were looking to engage the services of replacement wizard?"

That perked her right up. Born business-woman. Scary attribute in an aristocrat. "Oh, yes. I enquired with the Bey's staff. They approved the standard contract for services that Ubakh, in the kingdom of Azerdanshi, uses for wizards. Including the hazard pays and combat bonuses."

Did they now? Before or after you told them who you wanted to hire? Or would that be telling? "I see," I said. And I did. "If you have a copy, I can review it and let you know my thoughts."

"Of course," she agreed. She gave the half-orq, Hillevi, a nod. The girl, woman now that she was standing up and the cloak was out of the way, took a few steps in our direction. Much more politely, this time. Not bad looking either, if you liked them tough, green, and carnivorous. I had my days.

The dog looked up at me, perched on the floor with her paws under her. I shook my head. I didn't really know how smart the dog is, but she relaxed. Hillevi saw it too, and took one more step closer. So, smart, too. She extended a scroll tube in carved—something. Was that jade? Really? Damn. That was serious money right there.

"M'lady," she murmured. While her eyes were staring daggers at me over the girl's head. Which reminded me...

"M'Lady. I do not believe we have been properly introduced." I stood up from my stool, and bowed regally in court fashion. Hey, some skills you never lost. "I am Kaleph Sa'id, wizard extraordinaire, at your service."

She rose, and returned a very formal curtsy. Yep, definitely a noblewoman. I'd hurt myself trying that. "And I am the Lady Aurélie Sibylle d'Cienny, daughter of the Baron Chartre."

I took her hand, bowed over it, kissed it properly, and handed her back onto the rough wooden stool with one leg too short. Aga had joined Serkan hovering close by. The wine glasses were both full. The children were safely out of sight, so apparently Aga had been paying attention a few moments ago. If Serkan ever gets tired of his wonderful wife, I'd definitely take her. Smart.

Lady Aurélie passed me the jade scroll tube and returned to her wine. I controlled the urge to taste the jade to see if it was real. Popped open one end, slid out a hunk of parchment, set it carefully down where it wouldn't roll away on the uneven bar.

Sure enough. Standard Guild contract. Hadn't see one of those in years. Written in court Azerdanshi, even. All the usual clauses. Bonded employee of Lady Aurélie's adventuring company, rather than a federated member. Fairly normal for a newbie. Pay instead of a share of any treasure recovered. Hadn't changed much in the eight years since I last signed one. Pay rate of course blank, to be negotiated later.

I nodded at her sublimely. "I will, of course, need to have my barrister review it." Did I know any barristers? Here? "There remains only the pay rate to be determined, and the length of the contract." And brass tacks. "How long were you planning on exploring in the Empty Quarter? And what, in particular, were you looking for?"

Her eyes got that cagey look you generally only see on the older prostitutes. Or accountants. That meant things had just gotten interesting, Lady Aurélie?

She sucked in a long, slow breath. "That depends."

Yep, the magic words.

"Perhaps as long as six months. We have a very old map of the Lost Kingdom and want to explore some of the older and more remote places."

Meaning, places the Kipchak haven't looted bone dry yet because they're under sand or protected by one of the weird mutant thingees that live out there, or both. Wizard stuff necessary.

"Six months is reasonable," I said sagely. "Winter is nearly over now and you'll likely avoid the worst of the summer changestorms."

Nasty, nasty things. Magical vortex that sucked up all the eldritch power out of the over-saturated ground, piled it up in something that resembles a sandstorm, and warped the hell out of anybody or anything it rolled across. Most of the time, it would snap you back afterwards. If you were lucky. And sometimes, you ended up with a scorpion six feet tall. And hungry. And mean. "And your thoughts on pay?"

She marshalled her armies carefully in her mind. Somebody had taught this little aristocrat accounting. Rare in a noble. Rarer still to see training like that stick. "Based on the going rate, I believe a Beqdash Half-Crown would be appropriate and commensurate."

This was why I learned to play poker. The going rate from the Bey was about seven Dinars a day, not ten, but I wasn't about to give that tidbit away for free. The larger trading houses might go up to nine if they were desperate enough. I would have done it for six in my present circumstances.

In the end, my ego wouldn't settle for less than eleven. I was going to end up earning them, too.

And she named the dog Isabelle.

⌒

14th Day of Marh: Beqdash

Well, I have a job. Actual, real money. Bought Isabelle a nice collar and a day at the doggie spa. Got me some newer gear. The Empty Quarter is hot and rough and angry. Hasn't changed in the six years

I've been on this side of the water. Don't figure it ever will. But I have better equipment than the last time I tried this. And a couple of serious killers along for the ride. That's also an improvement.

Lady Aurélie fell in love with the Capering Camel and moved her whole troop here while she finalized details for the trip northeast into the badlands of the Empty Quarter. Keeps me from having to move and I get to see her team in action before we head out into unsafe places. Very interesting mix of very interesting characters.

I came downstairs for some oatmeal this morning to possibly the strangest sight I never expected to encounter.

The Kipchak tribes are almost universally Pucks from the eastern reaches beyond the low desert basin. So, three feet tall and exceedingly fierce. Chip on the shoulder types. They're the ones that have done the most exploring and looting in the areas of the Kyarajhum Desert to the east of Beqdash and the Empty Quarter north of that. Those were the two regions most damaged by the Desecration.

Hard, tough, mean places. The people turn out the same way.

Meanwhile, the Şimallı tribes tend to be humans or desert elves down from the north. True barbarians. Generally horsemen long on clan and tribe and ancestors, and short on patience for outsiders coming in and looting old tombs. Kipchak/Şimallı wars were frequent, and often bloody things. Like two packs of dogs arguing over a carcass. Bystanders beware.

I got to the bottom of the stairs like any other day, fairly early because I liked my morning peace, to sip fresh coffee imported from the distant southlands, and to think without a lot of noise around me.

Lady Aurélie had two locals she'd hired on her previous venture into the Empty Quarter last year.

Indril is a Puck. She's even tougher and harder and meaner than Hillevi is, which is saying something. And older than Hillevi, maybe twenty-five, so a prime warrior with a truncated two-handed battleblade. I watched her practicing yesterday on a training dummy in the rear courtyard. She was good. Really happy to have her between me and bad things.

The other local is a Şimallı boy named Brethard Wahyrst, and I do mean boy. Maybe fourteen. Apparently a total outcast who ran away from his clan rather than be one of them. This meant I already liked him to begin with. Not that I normally have anything nice to say about the barbarians. But the kid's apparently a first-rate scavenger and mountaineer, which means he's probably worth his weight in silver for what this group is doing.

This morning, as I looked around, and picked my jaw up off the floor, Indril was teaching Brethard to read. And she was teaching him Azerdanshi, which was a far more rare written language on this side of the Khazhar Sea. That a Kipchak could even read Azerdanshi was weird enough. I wasn't ready for a Şimallı Man of Letters. Call me old fashioned.

I staggered over to the bar and sat down next to Lady Aurélie's archer. He was, at once, the weirdest person in the group and the most refreshingly normal. But I suppose that most people weren't used to the Agama, as they weren't all that common this far north. You have to cross two major mountain ranges and a wonderfully-green plateau filled with crazy and occasionally cannibalistic tribesmen to get to the Agama homeland on the shores of the Southern Sea.

So a six foot tall lizardman with an orange mating crest sat at the bar, and drank juice of some kind, like the beginning of a bad joke. In between sips, he worked to sharpen a new batch of strange looking arrowheads.

I nodded at the two in the corner at their lessons. "What's the story there?"

One eye, reddish with purple flecks, turned enough my way to give me a glance before he went back to his drink. "It is an epic tale, the likes of which lowly markmen such as myself are rarely deigned worthy to consider the implications of, sir wizard. Mayhap you could endeavor to pursue such inquiries directly and thus feed our potential prurient desires for innuendo and ennui. I shall guard your rear flanks during such an encounter and protect whatever alcoholic beverages are left behind, that no sneaky thieves partake of them in your absence."

There was enough smile on his face that I knew better than to take him seriously, after I translated what he said.

Nobody took Ulene Dreamsailor seriously, not even himself. It worked out better for everyone that way.

Aga distracted me from following up by setting a bowl of hot oatmeal in front of me right then, along with a mug of coffee. I let it be and watched Ulene work. "How did you make those?"

He smiled at me and held up one of the arrowheads to catch the morning light. It was a swirl of light and dark metals that looked like a cake I had eaten once at one of the Bey's parties. "There is an indigenous metalsmith I have found," he said, "who swears on the efficacy of these implements for hunting fell creatures. He takes the time to hammer-forge low quality iron-steel and silver coins into a folded metal bloom before shaping them and welding on a shaft cup. According to local experts, that keeps the iron and silver separate and allows them to work better, because some the demons you find are vulnerable to silver and others to iron, but that alloy-mixing them will weaken the effects on either."

I nodded sagely. Never used iron or silver to do the job. Always had big dumb people with sharp things to handle it. And spells. "And does it work?"

"As of the present endeavor, I have been unable to arrange such a meeting to validate the theory." He smiled sideways at me and went back to sharpening them with a file.

I tried once again. "You can call me Kaleph. It is the name that I answer to most frequently."

"You have mentioned that, on more than one occasion, sir wizard. I am sure to give it great thought."

I gave up. The oatmeal was getting cool.

About halfway through breakfast, the morning got even more interesting. Hillevi, the demi-orq bodyguard chick, had been much more polite the last few days. Isabelle even liked her now. Enough to sit up and lick her hand as Hillevi sat down next to me opposite Ulene. I eyed her carefully sideways as I ate. Might as well make her do all the work. Took her a while to realize it.

"We need to talk."

If I had a Dinar for every time a woman had started a conversation with me that way, I wouldn't be living in Beqdash scratching out my survival in the desert. I could hear the barely-audible snicker from my other side as the archer concentrated on being invisible. Apparently, so could she.

"Let us go sit in the corner, where we can talk like civilized adults without an audience." I'll give her this, she was trying very hard not to react to all the snide and provocatory things I'd said in the last three days. Sometimes I couldn't help myself. Sometimes.

I turned to look right at her, studied her face with skills that made me a pretty good poker player, and nodded. "Lead on, madam." I grabbed my oatmeal and my coffee and followed her. Without her cloak on, it was a nice view.

She sat in the very corner to watch the whole room. I sat to one side, right at the edge of being uncomfortably, almost impolitely, close. Irritation makes people give things away and I had a feeling she was going to be one to watch. Isabelle curled up on the floor close by, watching the rest of the room and leaving me to deal with the half-orc. Still not sure how smart that dog was.

Hillevi didn't bother waiting for me to speak this time, or finish my breakfast. "The mistress requires," she began, "that we be on good terms, as members of a common team. I do not feel that you respect me."

Okay, blunt. I should have expected that from Hillevi. None of the rest of them could even walk a straight line, let alone talk one, when it came to being honest and forthright about this adventure, but she was going straight at the problem. Not normally the way I'd have done it, but she did get right to the point, which made it easier. I could play that.

"It's not that," I smiled around a mouthful of oatmeal. "I don't respect her." That got a rise out of her, until I pointed the dirty spoon in her face like a baton as she started to stand. "Oh, I respect her money. And her rank. And her brains. I'm sure she speaks several more languages than I do, and better. She does not, however, appear to have a lick of common sense, nor does that librarian." I let that dangle for a moment, like that last drop of honey. "I presume that's what you're for."

A fish will make that same motion. Mouth opening. Mouth closing. Opening again. I refrained from checking to see if she had gills to wiggle, since I was about two bites to the bottom of my oatmeal. I got there before her brain got sorted out, so I continued.

"Your job is to protect her from big, bad, mean things, and you think I'm a threat, right?"

She nodded, warily, cagily. Apparently not the morning she had in mind when she got up, either. Good.

"I'm safe," I said. "I like grown-ups. She's a spoiled little princess with money playing at being an adventurer, not a merciless killer equipped to master the Empty Quarter."

We sat in stunned silence long enough for me to loot a good deal of my coffee. Aga makes the best coffee in town. Finally, Hillevi stirred.

"Then why did you take the job, oh great and powerful sorcerer?" Sarcastic women do something extra for me. This demi-orq was going to be trouble. But hey, they all were. And she wanted an honest answer now. Save us all a lot of heartburn later.

"Because, for a kid, she impresses the hell out of me with her ability to organize things. Get things done. Have you looked at the group you travel with? I mean, really looked at them? You've got a Kipchak teaching a Simalli to read over there. An Agama. The librarian, Melisande, speaks more languages than I've heard of. One of the best camel-masters in Beqdash. And you. Plus she hired me." She was back to making the fish motions. I let her. Another sip of coffee. "And this is your second season in the Empty Quarter. She's, what, eighteen? Nineteen?"

"Eighteen," came the quiet response after a few moments.

"Right, so at sixteen, she decides to go adventuring, puts together a very competent team of experts, transports them three thousand miles across several seas, and makes it home without losing anyone. Which reminds me, just how did your first wizard, one Homas Beminster, manage to drown in a desert town?"

"Oh." The eyes got a whole new level of scrutiny now. "You'll have to ask the Mistress that." More study. Like maybe actually looking at me for the first time as a person instead of a threat. "Who are you, Kaleph Sa'id the sorcerer?"

My coffee was empty. I rose to go get more. "A man who has a job to do, Mistress Hillevi. Good day."

When I got to the bar, I handed Aga my cup for more and took up my seat next to Ulene. Hillevi probably didn't realize how good the average Agama's hearing was. I knew better. Ulene glanced at the corner and then smiled at me.

I glanced at him, turned my attention back to fresh coffee. "She still sitting there?"

"Indeed, master wizard, indeed." He grinned. "Be careful that that one does not get it into her head that she must marry you."

That brought my head around. "Not my type, Ulene Dreamsailor."

He chuckled. "Oh, silly human. Like that would stop a woman like her once she got such a notion firmly implanted in her consciousness."

I looked over my shoulder at her and considered throwing myself under a chariot. "No, seriously, Ulene. She's all yours."

"Hush, you." He went back to sharpening. And grinning.

19th Day of Marh: North of Beqdash

It's hot. Dry, nasty, brutal hot. Which makes it nice, considering the alternative is one of those sudden, late-season rain storms off the Khazhar Sea, or worse, a changestorm down from the north. Really don't want to face another one of those.

We're two and half days out of Beqdash on the old northern road that used to be the main trade artery along the Khazar Sea in the days of the Lost Kingdom. Seven adventurers camelback, one camel master and six assistants, and about thirty of the big smelly beasts bearing people or gear. Feels more like a caravan than a combat exploration, but we've got enough people to do both.

And one big, happy dog. I swear, she's on a grand jaunt, ears up, tail flapping happily, running over to sniff a cactus or chase a shrew. Obviously not a city dog. She's home.

I wandered around the Empty Quarter in my memory, placing landmarks against entropy. Not much had changed. Nor likely to, although I had heard rumors of a cabal of druids from the southwest who had made it their life's work to make the desert bloom again. Have to kill off all the big nasty mutant things running around first, but I supposed that was where people like us came in, anyway. The monsters protected the valuable things. We wanted the loot. Eventually, we would win and the druids could tend to wastelands in peace.

Eventually, civilized folk will spill out of Beqdash and fill up the Quarter as well. As soon as Beqdash accumulates enough civilized folk. Not holding my breath on that one. Still, the road was a little less *something* than it had been. A few more gnarled little trees and desert scrub than I remember from last time. Hell, I might live long enough to see it bloom.

Ahead of me, I watched Lady Aurélie and her librarian, Melisande Brottie, consult the map. The Map. For all the noble lady was a shrewd businesswoman, the librarian was a hothouse rose. Not that you needed hothouses around Beqdash, but then, nobody was from Beqdash. But they'd all seen one. A hothouse rose, that is. Desperately intellectual little elf girl. Almost a pixie with her blond page-boy hair and washed out blue eyes. Always looked like she was about to fall off the camel. Or trip over her own feet. And yet, probably older than anyone here, at least in human years. Still a kid in elf terms. Could read at least eleven languages, which was far better than I could do, although I could usually unravel anything magically, given enough time. And, she only spoke three, and nothing east of Court Azerdanshi.

Apparently, something interesting on the map. Lady Aurélie called a rest break and asked the camelmaster to set up a shelter. Kysndar and his boys went right to work while I kneeled my camel down and drank some well-wined water. Isabelle curled up in the camel shade for a dish of water and a couple bites of smoked eel while I updated the journal.

After about long enough to start getting antsy, I decided to wander up and see if I could help. After all, this only was their second trip east of the Khazhar Sea, and I've been here for years.

However, apparently that was a Bad Idea.

Isabelle bounced up next to the two ladies and got their attention. Lady Aurélie took one look at me and immediately folded the map closed and gave me a tight look. Didn't say anything. Just stared at me. Hard. Unwelcoming. After a while, you could learn enough female body language from experience to recognize these things.

I decided to play it nonchalant. I nodded politely. "Ladies. Just enquiring if you had any need for my experience or expertise in the desert."

Hillevi stood close by and gave me a pleading look, a tight smile. Aurélie scowled effectively. After a moment, her brain engaged, or her manners, one of the two. "No, thank you, Mr. Sa'id. That won't be necessary. We'll let you know."

Ouch. Okay, then. I moved on.

Ulene was keeping watch from atop a small tor beside the road that was generally known as Ulvi's Watch. Famous place. Good view in every direction. Put an archer like him up there and you could have great peace of mind. Nobody was getting close without being seen. I climbed up to sit next to him and enjoy the sun. My darker skin does far better than the fair-skinned westerners. And a scaly Agama like Ulene appeared to be in heaven.

Isabelle plopped down beside us, tail keeping the beat as I scanned the horizon.

Irrepressible smiled at me and scratched Isabelle behind one ear. "And how is our bon wizard enjoying the flat desert heat and boundless sky on this otherwise lovely day?"

I scowled sourly in his general direction. "Fine. Absolutely, positively wonderful."

"That is very good, oh great sorcerous thread-weaver. I had feared that the rather-perverse behaviors of our two leading ladies might have combined to produce a negative outlook in your overall perspective this day. It exhilarates me that you do not take such things to heart."

If I thought it would work, I'd have given him the stinkeye, but the effort would have been wasted there. I settled for a non-denominational grunt in reply.

Ulene plowed on. I'd learned him well enough by then to realize how keen his insights were, so he was just having fun with me at this point. But it was harmless fun. "Perhaps, Master Sa'id the well-known enchanter of dead tribal savages and illusionary trolls, you are trapped in a situation with a headstrong female-type who rejects your honest overtures when she cannot distinguish them from your sarcastic genuflections?"

I eyed him closely. "It would be nice to be listened to. I do have some useful ideas and experience out here."

He smiled sidelong at me with a wink. "Perhaps. But you are, as you are no doubt well aware, a potent and unknown force to them. Whose services were an involuntary necessity engendered by the sudden and unexpected demise of her favorite teacher and near-uncle of a wizard. And you do children's shows, something the dread Beminster would not have been caught dead unleashing on a public spectacle."

I shrugged. "So my problem is that I'm not serious enough to impress her?"

Ulene shrugged. "Unlikely, formidable spell-binder. We have all heard the story of how you came to know Isabelle. You do not, however, tend to comport yourself with the dignity and gravitas of your supposed rank, at least in the eyes of the two aristocrats to whom such things matter. Being myself just a lowly hired sword of alien background, the importance of such trivialities are apparently lost on my lesser understandings of human interactions."

I looked at him sidelong as my eyes scanned the horizon. Old habit out here. Good one. "Uh-huh."

I watched Ulene surge to his feet and shade his eyes with his draw hand. I was standing next to him a moment later. Even Isabelle popped up to sniff.

Even serious, the Agama was circuitous. "Unlike the most-esteemed ladies who represent executive authority during our travels and travails, I am not above requesting the assistance of such lesser genders as yourself in identifying such wayward and untoward desert signals as those visible on the northern horizon. Pray tell, master magus, what does your long and checkered past inform you about such things?"

I considered getting him drunk. Not that it would shut him up, but it might make him loosen up enough that it didn't hurt my head to unravel his conversations. In his case, it would probably make him worse. Right now, I didn't need worse.

Damn, his eyes were really good. I would have mistaken it for a cloud or something. Even after I grabbed a small thread of magic and wove it into something to make my eyes sharper. But it was there. Growing.

The desert tongues have so much more interesting ways to curse than even a flowery language like Court Azerdanshi. In my head, I was exploring them. And probably muttering them under my breath for the quiet snickers I was getting from Ulene.

I released the thread so I could focus on the archer with a very serious scowl. Even a single raised eyebrow on his part was somehow more eloquent than anything I could say at this point. The slight cock of his head was just icing. Brutal, bitchy icing.

I smiled. Bad luck sometimes goes down better with a smile. Even a grim one. "That, my jade friend, is a changestorm."

Not that I wanted to actually experience everything else, but watching his irrepressible nature actually sag helped my humor. But then, I have a small soul. Misery loves company.

I watched it for a few more heartbeats, just to be sure. Yup. Inbound. In my head, I spun a map around. Ulvi's Watch was on the western edge of some badlands. Nothing so useful as a mountain within a day's ride, but hopefully the rough ground would help shield us. It works on tornadoes, right?

I heard Ulene a step behind me as I scrambled down the short trail and leapt the last few feet onto the roadway. Isabelle was close behind.

Ahead, I watched Lady Aurélie and her librarian look up from their damnable map again. Her look turned even more sour as she realized I was coming over to talk to her. It got a touch nervous when she realized I was running. It really bubbled when she realized Ulene Dreamsailor, that phlegmatic philosopher and dread sniper, was running right behind me.

We all three skidded to a halt close to the two aristocratic teenagers. Even in a panic, I could never resist. I took a moment to perform a full court bow commensurate with her rank. I could be a shit, sometimes, but today, she deserved it a little. "M'lady, not knowing many of the details of your former adventures in the desert vastness of the Empty Quarter, I will simply report the news. There's a changestorm coming. A big one. Right at us."

In that moment, something good could have been born. Something bright and shiny. A solid foundation of trust and reliance upon which to base our ongoing relationship. Happy times.

Instead, she turned to the archer. "What is this fool babbling about?"

Hillevi, at least, had the decency to wince, invisible behind them.

Right now, I wished I could do that thing where you put two fingers in your mouth and make a sound audible a half mile away. I clapped my hands together really hard a few times to get heads turned this way. "Whyren. Changestorm from the north. Fast one. Big."

That was rewarded with a proper amount of panic on his part. Someone believed me. And he could whistle. And he had well-trained camel drivers. They had the pack beasts up and ready to move in seconds. The westerners were still processing things when I turned back.

Melisande, the librarian, turned an even paler shade of elf. She was really going to need a better hat and long sleeves if she stayed out in the sun much longer. "A changestorm? Really? But they are out of season."

I cocked my head at her, kinda like the way Isabelle watched me occasionally. "Madam Brottie, they do not have a season. They are more frequent in the winter months for reasons unknown to modern arcana, but can and do happen any time of year."

Lady Aurélie looked like she had bitten a particularly sour lime. One of the good ones like they grew on the southern shores of the Khazhar Sea, not the little dwarfs the merchants sold in Beqdash. I smiled at my executrix innocently and waited.

I'll give her this. When she went into tactical mode, she was an absolute dervish. A born general. If she were to take up the military as a hobby with the same verve and competence as she went looting in the deserts, there were going to be a few unstable crowns in the far West. I would travel that far just to watch her take on the silly people back home. Some serious apple-cart upsetting in that woman's future.

I stepped back as she unleashed her own personal whirlwind. The camel-master and his crew was already in motion, so I started towards mine, with Isabelle out front. Figured she could handle it.

I got about two steps when I felt a hand on my elbow. Well, maybe more of a hook. Who knew a woman who weighed so little could put such force and gravitas into a simple grab of the arm. Whatever, she stopped me cold and stepped close enough to speak without anyone hearing. "Sa'id, what's the safest direction to escape?"

Nothing more. No histrionics. No feminine wiles. Just cold, hard, calculating, professional. I returned her hard look for a second, saw the hard woman she could become when push came to shove relax into a smart leader willing to ask advice. Damn it. Just when I was all set to start hating her, too.

I leaned closer. Not close enough to kiss her, heaven forbid such insouciance from one of the masses, but she had apparently chewed mint leaves after breakfast. "Due east. Into the badlands and hope we find a wadi or a box canyon to shelter in."

I could see the calculations in her eyes. She decided. "You take point. Find us a place."

I blinked in utter shock and stood there dumb-founded for a moment. Or, more dumb-founded than usual around smart women.

She actually grinned at me for a just a flash of a moment. Bright, warm, intimate. Damn it.

After another beat, she turned and started issuing orders that got everyone in motion. I hung for a second longer, gathered the shards of my misconceptions and stuffed them into a metaphorical pocket before I loped over to my camel and mounted.

I had never figured out how smart the dog was. Way smarter than she should be. I decided to play a hunch. You never knew. She'd been out here more than any of us, after all. "Isabelle. Changestorm. Find shelter."

She cocked her head at me, like normal when I do something human, and then turned and sniffed the air, facing due north, right into the teeth of it. Good nose. She growled under her breath and took off to her right, up a small embankment. Isabelle stopped there and looked down at the rest of us before woofing once loudly and dropping down the other side.

Oh, what the hell. I put spur and crop to my beast and headed up the slope after Isabelle. She at least seemed to know what she was doing.

I was glad one of us did.

I watched Isabelle stop as she crested every rise or passed every notch with a view to her left. I could smell the changestorm coming closer. It felt like a sandstorm, but all the magic in it made it feel wetter, like one of the nasty winter rainstorms that squalled across the Khazhar Sea on a bad day.

It was going to be a bad day here, too.

The whole northern horizon was black now. Behind me, I could see the rest of the troupe strung out like big fuzzy pearls as different camels had different opinions about things. Ulene was closest. Partly, that was because it was his job. Hillevi was a bit back, with Lady Aurélie and Ms. Brottie just behind her and the rest strung out from there. Indril, the puck, was last, but that appeared to be by choice, to keep anyone from overtaking us. I was good with that. I was having enough trouble keeping my own camel from doing something stupid and bolting.

The ground was definitely getting rougher. I was following Isabelle down something someone might charitably call a wadi, if pressed. It was about five camels wide and almost deep enough that my head was below the line of the rising winds, but I was tall, so the others might have been shielded behind me. Wasn't about to take the time to ask. Isabelle was getting excited ahead of me, so hopefully this little ditch was turning into something more useful up ahead. I kept forgetting that the gods have a sense of humor.

Isabelle disappeared around a bend as the sidewalls suddenly swept upwards. This felt like a nifty little box canyon. Good.

We would be in deep camel dung if rains triggered any flashfloods, but I couldn't remember any story about rain in a changestorm. Just as well. It was bad enough.

I was in the middle of them before I realized someone was already there. I was also right about this being a nice little box canyon. Not so bad as to be a trap, but more than enough to keep the camels from getting up the sides easily.

Fortunately, they were just as surprised as I was. Nobody had any weapons out. Yet.

Isabelle sat on the far side of the tiny Şimallı encampment, tail wagging and surrounded by about a dozen tribesmen. No women, so this wasn't a clan group. Probably a raiding party. Bad news. They were awfully close to Beqdash, too, so they couldn't have been up to any good. She happily woofed at me as I came into view and tried to stop my landship of a camel before I went aground on anybody. Barely. And then the beast settled. So much for escape.

Heads came around. Happy smiles suddenly got downright cold. Mutterings could be heard over the wind. Hands found blades and started pulling them out.

Crap. Lone travelers don't fare well on the high desert. Folks like these were why.

Normally, I could wiggle my way out of things like this, either with a glib tongue or a show magical enough might impress them enough to buy me space. I looked down at my left hand and tried one of the simplest tricks I know. My fingernails grew half an inch and my entire hand turned purple with green polka-dots. Yup, changestorm.

One of them smiled at me. It was a happy smile, for him. A "son, you walked into the wrong place, today..." kind of smile. He drew a nasty little sword from his belt and took a step forward. The others did the same.

Isabelle didn't move, which surprised me. Maybe my enchantments were warping in the storm and she had started to revert to the vicious killing machine she was when I met her. That would have been just marvelous. Eleven on one would be twelve on one. Then they all froze and stopped smiling. Eleven on two, it seems.

If he'd been close enough, I would have kissed him. Seriously. Nobody else can do such justice to Azerdanshi. It was like finding a hidden well with cold water after three days of heat. "Oh great sorcerous ambassador to the dread heathens of the untamed north, perhaps you could induce your new friends to politely put away all their deadly paraphernalia and comport themselves over to one side of yon encampment before I am required by the failing of my own linguistic studies to convey such a simple point in a much less friendly and perhaps messier manner?"

I climbed off my sedentary beast and smiled warmly at the Şimallı in front of me, specifically the one I figured to be the leader. On my right, Ulene Dreamsailor stood on his beast with that nasty greatbow drawn and pointed at the guy. Two spare arrows waited in the fingers of his bow-hand, plus one in his teeth. The Agama was smiling the same smile they seemed to have forgotten, just a few heartbeats ago. It looked much nicer on him, but that was because I was suddenly going to live through the next few moments. Hopefully.

Isabelle bounced over and plopped down next to my camel, looking like the cat that ate the canary. She didn't just set up a distraction and ambush on her own, did she?

Did she?

I looked at my left hand again and considered the situation. I was worthless in close combat, but they didn't know that. Ulene would slaughter at least half of them if they did anything stupid at this moment. They seemed to understand that much. Stalemate. And then heads turned away from us.

I risked a quick glance and saw Lady Aurélie and Hillevi just inside the mouth of the canyon with crossbows loaded. Where had those come from? I needed to remember to ask, later. And not play poker with that woman for real money any time soon.

The guy in charge over there decided to play for time. "What is the meaning of this? Are you brigands to prey upon innocent travelers?"

You had to admire brass like that. I wasn't about to cut him a moment of slack, but it was nice dealing with someone who had more brains than the last two tribesmen I'd run into, back in Beqdash.

It also dawned on me that nobody in the group but me could communicate with this group in anything beyond rudimentary terms.

Brottie hadn't learned the tongues of the Empty Quarter, though she would, given time, and Lady Aurélie only knew a few words.

Body language counted though. Right now, she was conveying to them the importance of earnest politeness. Difficult to do with a crossbow, but that's what made her a noblewoman, I supposed. I glanced over at Isabelle, and caught her smile. How smart was my dog, anyway?

I cocked my head and smiled at the guy. It was a warm, friendly, *Don't do anything stupid or I'll crack your long bones for the marrow* kind of look. Şimallı weren't known for being subtle. "Greetings. My companions and I are currently seeking shelter. There is a changestorm coming. This seems like a very good place to ride it out."

He wasn't too pleased with that idea. But he also wasn't suicidal. His hands stayed in plain sight. Point for our side. "We were already here. You should ride on and find someplace else."

Normally, I'd have agreed, but the hairs on the back of my neck were standing up. Not because of him. That storm was going to be a doozy, and it was almost on top of us. "There's no time. If you move to that side, we will stay over here and everyone can obey the laws of the oasis."

He was too canny to do anything stupid, at least yet. We had gotten the drop on them with the help of a canny canine, and we outnumbered them, although they didn't realize how few true killers were in our group. Plus, only fools fought in a burning house.

On the other side of the ledger, we were obviously city folk. They had special terms for people from Beqdash and beyond. None of them were polite in mixed company. And they'd really be upset if they discovered that our leader was a teenage girl. Unmarried was going to be bad enough. Educated was likely to piss them off. Too much like the Azerdanshi.

Heartbeats passed.

He finally decided I wasn't bluffing.

I wasn't, but they couldn't know without testing Ulene's skill. I would have been comfortable with that. Between him and the women with crossbows, it would have been a slaughter. Indril tossed into the mix, a Kipchak woman with a two-handed sword facing her culture's worst enemies, and they might have tried something on general principle. But they also would have been annihilated. She played rough.

My kind of woman, even if I generally liked them more than three feet tall.

Hetman over there raised his hands well away from his sides and said something to his men. Most of them did the same. One protested. I couldn't hear what he said, because the winds were getting really nasty, but the guy in charge over there barked something and pointed at Ulene. Punk kid looked at the archer and raised his hands as well.

It was so nice to be on the winning side of this equation. For once.

⸻

This wasn't the first changestorm I'd ever endured, but it might be the first one I've ever had pass right over me. It was like sitting at the bottom of a well while someone dropped marbles on you one at a time. None of them hurt, but they stung. Best way to describe it to a mundane would like your whole body fell asleep and tingled, instead of just the arm you were sleeping on. For an hour. So far. One of the reasons I tried to stay in Beqdash unless someone was paying me well to come out here.

Changestorms never made it as far as the city. The Bey always claimed it was a result of the work of his sorcerers to protect the palace. I knew better, having been one of them, once upon a time.

For the last little while, the winds had come down out of the north hard. The scrub and badlands around us broke some of it up, but that just mostly just kept the sands from polishing my downwind side clean and smooth. Isabelle was hard in tight against the side of my camel, head and tail tucked under. I'm not nearly that limber. Plus, I wanted to keep a clear view of things.

Across the way, Hetman and his troupe waited. It turned out his name was Amarjeet, so he was an even longer ways from home than I expected. They had kept their camels behind them and close against the canyon wall, presumably to keep us from stealing anything. Whatever.

Ulene and Indril kept a kind of watch. Apparently, Agama were largely immune to the effects of all this magical static swirling around, and Indril's about as mundane as a brick. Everyone else was heads-down trying to stay out of the way and hoping they didn't get zapped by anything as the winds swirled and tugged.

I was practically vibrating with static electricity. So much so that I had to clench my jaw tight and practically sit on my hands not to work any threads, even by accident. This was going to turn into a massive migraine in a couple of hours, unless the backside of the storm sucked all the nastiness back out.

I wasn't holding my breath on that one. Last one hadn't. Privilege of all the other fun stuff I got to do. Or penance. The Gods had a black sense of humor.

In retrospect, I should have known Amarjeet and his friends would try something. This wasn't my first foray into the Empty Quarter. But I was having a hard time stringing snarky comments together inside my own head, let along keep up my half of any proverbial conversation.

The winds had built up to a good head of steam. The Inner Sea, far to the west, was big enough to have actual tides. I'd never swum in it, but I sat on a cliff-face one afternoon drinking the local distillate with some friends watching the bay empty nearly completely out, and then refill. It was like watching a bathtub move.

This was the same, only with wind instead of water.

A huge surge of winds came down off the ledge behind me like an assassin, left me and everyone else blind for a few seconds.

Amarjeet and his crew took off at a dead run, right at us.

Ulene wasn't surprised, his second eyelids worked just fine. But his first arrow went almost straight up off his bow as the sirocco took it. And then he disappeared under three or four of the tribesmen. Indril got proper respect. Six men, all of them twice her size, dog-piled her and held on. They were barely enough. The other four were on Hillevi and Lady Aurélie before they knew what was happening, blades out and threatening.

I nursed the world's worst hangover and tried to think.

Lady Aurélie cursed as her hands were bound.

Amarjeet laughed.

Indril got good and hogtied.

Hillevi kicked and fussed until someone growled at her.

They came for me last, which made sense, since I was about as threatening as a two-day-old kitten at this point. Apparently, it was possible to get drunk on a changestorm. Weirder crap had happened. I laughed out loud.

Lady Aurélie's voice penetrated. "Sa'id, you worthless cur, do something."

"Lady, I'm having a hard enough time not doing anything. You want to get us all killed? You're in charge. Do something yourself."

Crap. Did I say out loud? Must have, heads were turned my direction. Jaws had dropped.

Amarjeet stood over me and laughed some more. I joined him, although mine sounded a lot more hysterical, or maniacal. Hard to separate the two.

She tried again, but I was hearing her through the soft-padded walls of a bordello. *Why was the air fuzzy?* "Kaleph. KALEPH."

Hey, that was my name. I goggled in her direction as Amarjeet grabbed me by the lapels and lifted me to my feet. Or, at least close to my feet. The planet kept tilting. *Damned ground. Stand still.* "What?"

At this range, it looked like a good approximation of the stinkeye I occasionally got across the bar from attractive women. Hard to tell in this wind. And my drunken state.

Anyway, Lady Aurélie did something with her face that got me focused. Or at least squinting in her direction. Close enough. "You were hired to do a job. I expect you to fulfill your contract."

Ouch. Even punchdrunk on changestorm, that made it through the layer of fuzzy oblivion in my head. Clearly, though, this woman was insane. Cast a spell in the middle of a changestorm? Hell, breathing is almost enough to cast something. Not a chance, lady.

And then Amarjeet screwed up.

He turned and snapped his fingers at one of the men holding Aurélie's hands.

That man reached up and growled at her to be quiet. And then he hit her.

That wasn't right. There were ladies present. Someone needed better manners.

What to do? What to do?

Oh hell. Let's go out in a blaze of stupid.

I studied the three Amarjeets in front of me. All of them were pug-ugly. None of them were paying any attention to the drunk wizard. I reached out and touched his breastbone.

It's a changestorm. Let's change. Yippee!

Okay, maybe that was possibly the dumbest thing I'd ever done, in retrospect. Even worse than that one time at the Bey's birthday celebration.

But it worked.

Of course, that one worked too. Just got me fired. And blackballed. Noblemen, *fah.*

I'd never had a changestorm fill me with this much power before. It felt really good, except I had a feeling like I had to pee and it wasn't going to come out that easily. Otherwise, I'd have tried, believe me.

But, lightning rods work. Even against magical lightning bolts.

Let's try it here.

Amarjeet wasn't trying to dodge me. Hell, he had to hold me to keep me upright. And my arms were longer.

So I touched him.

And grounded the biggest thread I could grab from the cyclone of crazy energy crackling invisibly around me. It kinda looked like a giant anthill.

Boy, was he surprised.

He started off angry. They tend to be, on the downwind side of a good practical joke. Şimallı tribal barbarian chief-types have no sense of humor. None.

Then he turned blue. Not a blueish tinge to otherwise pink skin. Not sky blue. Nope. That dark, nasty blue of the Khazhar Sea as the storm is building up. *Yup.*

And then the changestorm found my lightning rod.

According to the kid, Brethard, that was when the screaming started. I didn't really remember much in any sort of coherent narrative. Flashes of silliness and color, like soap bubbles on a summer day. Maniacal laughter. Apparently, most of that was mine. Then a zolt of something good grounding.

Tore the daylight entirely in half, right down the middle.

I looked this morning and there was still a spot on the ground over there where the sands had been flash-fried to shattered glass crystals. *Groovy.*

Amarjeet became one with the changestorm. And my sense of indignant silliness. Turning him into a newt would have been child's play at that point, with this much power floating around. I decided to turn that rat bastard chauvinistic pig into a Şimallı warrior's worst nightmare.

A woman.

And not just any woman. Xedli, the six-armed Goddess of Plague and Destruction. A nightmare from Amarjeet's homeland.

And twelve feet tall. Because, why the hell not?

I remember her picking me up and screaming in rage. And I remember giggling a lot. It was the funniest thing in the world. I don't remember much after that. The others had to fill me in on the rest of the details. They might have been lying.

That old wives' tale about drunks falling down a flight of stairs and not getting hurt held water here, too. The kid said that Amarjeet-as-Xedli threw me at a camel.

I had no recollection and nothing to show for it except a small horseshoe-shaped bruise on my left arm, about three inches across. But apparently, it was awesome.

I considered doing some post-cognition spells to see everything, but my head hurt too much this morning. I settled for the kid's version, interspersed with Indril's giggling observations. Who knew that a puck swordmistress had such a wicked sense of humor?

So, Amarjeet-as-Xedli threw me at a camel. Not the worst thing a woman has done to me, even this month. Then she turned on everyone else and began howling in Şimallı.

Since nobody here spoke it but me, whatever pithy observations were made were lost. But it was apparently good.

Or Şimallı are just the most superstitious bastards in the world. They attacked her.

Did I mention that she was twelve feet tall with six arms? Must have been like attacking a feeding frenzy of sharks. This morning, I found blood splatters on a wall, eight feet up, twenty feet away. Didn't belong to any of us.

That normally-overly-loquacious Agama, Ulene Dreamsailor, master archer, and scourge of the southern plateau, summed up the whole altercation with a single word. Personally, I'd have bet money he was incapable of doing that, but I've lost better odds.

I had looked at him and asked what happened after the tribesmen got themselves sorted out, since apparently Xedli lost. My morning coffee had finally started to cut through the layers of gunk and hangover piled on top of my mind.

He just blinked at me twice and gave me the oddest smile. "Indril."

When I looked in her direction, she had a smile of a cat that had eaten every canary in Beqdash.

Apparently it was possible for a three-foot-two puck to look nine feet tall. Glad she was on my side.

By the time I got to the tin at the bottom of the coffee cup, Lady Aurélie made an appearance, trailed by Brottie and Hillevi.

She sat across from me with the stillness of a woman decades older. Eyed me closely. Isabelle curled up across my lap a little closer, slow thumps from her tail. That got a scritch from the noblewoman.

"How much of yesterday do you remember, Sa'id?"

My head hurt. Parts of me were still numb that morning. I felt like I had run here from Beqdash.

She nodded. "I suspected as much."

Crap. And apparently I'm muttering out loud, too. Inner voice only, please.

I took an extra deep breath and tried to blow all the leftovers away. The words were almost a whisper. "Do you understand now, what a changestorm can do?"

She nodded. Again, the calm stillness of a much older woman. Dangerous. Crowns were going to roll, one of these days. "Today? Yes. Yesterday? I was furious at you for not protecting us. And then I watched you pick up a camel and move it out of your way."

I WHAT?

Numbed shock seemed appropriate. I practiced it some more.

She leaned forward. Not intimate. Secret. "What could you have done with that much power?"

Decades of glib sarcasm bubbled just below the surface. They always did. Today wasn't the time, nor the place. This child, this woman, demanded more. So be it. I leaned forward a bit as well. Again, not intimate. Secret. "Died. I almost did that anyway."

I felt her nod. We were close enough now that a kiss was a few degrees of inward separation, physically. Miles, emotionally. "So, Sa'id. Would you like to know why we're here?"

I nodded back. Jasmine. This morning, she had added a scent that wasn't there normally. Really? Was seducing me on the list of tools this morning? She certainly didn't like me that much. Did she? Besides, I wanted trust, not a roll in the sand.

I heard the traces of victory creep into her voice. "We're looking for the Rose Diamond."

Fortunately, for me, she leaned back as she whispered those words, or I would have broken my nose on her cheekbone when my head snapped around to stare at her.

Really?

You want to find the very artifact that obliterated the Desecration in the first place and killed hundreds of thousands of people? The source of the legend? The dark wizard who sought immortality for himself and the kidnapped princess, only to be destroyed when the shiny, handsome paladin arrived and screwed up the rescue? You want that?

I felt my head turn involuntarily to the northeast. I knew where to look. Every spellcaster with an ounce of power had felt the echoes of the Desecration at one time or another, like ripples from the middle of a still pond. It was still out there, pulsing, waiting. Some idiot would find it, someday.

And I knew why she needed a wizard to replace that idiot Beminster.

Bloodhound. And all the dark power that protected it now. Possibly true gods.

She sat there and watched me, perfectly still. Beautiful blue eyes. Lustrous brown hair braided against the wind. Calm. Rational. Executive.

And I realized I was dealing with the most dangerous creature known to man.

A competent romantic.

I was doomed.

At least Isabelle still loved me.

My favorite half-troll is back. And he is beginning to accumulate the regalia that he will have with him when Lord Admiral Brak, Warden of the Western Reaches, becomes a force to be reckoned with. It was a silly campaign, filled with silly players and silly characters, but it was also a place where a half-wit half-troll could aspire to be a god. Join me on the quest.

Destiny

Sleipnir paused to take in the combat scene before him as he reloaded his heavy crossbow. The Araneae warrior was at a distinct disadvantage in the close quarters of the tower's entryway, so he had stayed back, just outside the now-opened front door. The fading dusk outside made the view just that much more difficult inside, as oil-fired lamps in the hallway flickered and cast strange moving shadows.

He braced all eight of his feet, leaned back over his lower-body thorax like a rearing horse, popped up on his tip-toes, and looked over the mess in front of him through the oversized doorway. Better. He had a tactical view unmatched by people whose eyes were only three to six feet off the ground.

No good targets stood out though. Up front, Brak, his half-troll companion, swept skeletons into kindling with his humongous axe, *Woodchuck*. From here, Sleipnir could hear bits of some trollish ditty being hummed as he laid about him like a lumberjack, accentuated by the brittle shattering of bones.

Farther back, Princess, the Night Elf, fired the occasional arrow, using her naturally dark skin and black clothing to blend in with the ebon stone of the hallway. Sleipnir could see his human leader, Bob, offering suggestions to her from the middle of the hallway, and to the two-and-a-half-foot tall Puck wizard on Bob's other side. Piper's sorcery was having the most effect, but Sleipnir could see that it was a result of him thwarting the spell-casting efforts of their necromancer foe at the far end of the hall.

From his tip-toes, Sleipnir caught movement beyond the half-dozen skeletons left in the fight. "Bob," he yelled, "bad guy's making a break for it. The necromancer's running."

Bob turned to look back, his unblooded cutlass in one hand and an undamaged shield in the other. He blinked, looked up, then up again, to meet the Araneae warrior's eyes behind him, head nearly twelve feet off the ground. Sleipnir could see Bob's mind cycle through choices, implications, and estimations. Bob's ability to think quickly had kept them all alive many times. He arrived at one now from the flimsiest of evidence. "He's going upstairs where he can bar a door and summon more nasty things. You go up the outside of the tower and stop him. I'll send Brak to distract him from the front."

Sleipnir skittered backwards out of the entryway to the tower and glanced up at the stone face before him. He took the moment to reload his black crossbow and set the safety as he reached out with his front pair of spider feet and caught onto the brick. Slowly, he shifted himself vertical and began to climb up the side of the tower, just as the spider his lower half resembled would do.

∿

Bob pivoted back to the mission at hand as his Araneae scout disappeared up the outside of the tower. "Princess, go to close combat. Now." She glanced over as he stepped forward, heard her toss her bow back safely out of the way, heard her draw a pair of short blades.

Bob could see the necromancer fiddle to open a previously-hidden doorway to one side of the hallway and start to step through it. Up ahead, Bob watched as his half-troll destroyer shattered another skeleton. "Brak, ignore the skeletons and go after the wizard, right now. Don't let him get away or summon any more help, whatever you do. Stop him at any cost. We'll handle the rest."

Bob saw the great bearded head look back, saw the troll-kin warrior nod, and watched the seven-and-a-half-foot tall half-troll rush forward and grab a skeleton by the neck as he went by. Brak dashed the thing to pieces against a nearby wall as he raced to the closing door and stuck his great two-headed axe, *Woodchuck*, into the sill before the door could close.

Sleipnir peeked into a balcony window with all the noise of a church mouse. This floor looked like a dainty salon for entertaining guests, so he slowly ascended another level, carefully gripping bricks with his spidery toes as he circled the exterior. Most of the time, the loss of his true elven body was a point of great pain and indignity, but, occasionally, the new half-spider centaur shape had its uses. Not enough to make up for so failing the Dark Goddess, but...less bad.

The next floor up was an arcana library filled with all manner of books and trinkets and exotic weapons in fancy racks. Across the open space, Sleipnir saw the necromancer emerge from a staircase, holding a gnarled wooden staff with a glowing red orb attached to the top. The man held it horizontally above his head with both hands and began to chant in some unknown tongue as he crossed the room. Confident that he was invisible against the night sky behind him, Sleipnir shifted around to line up a killing shot.

A rumble of feet pounding up the stairs caused the necromancer to turn and look the other direction. Brak emerged from the stairwell at a dead run and howled some trollish insults at the man. The half-troll also blocked Sleipnir's shot, just as the crimson orb suddenly flared and filled the room with an unholy light.

What happened next would stay with the Araneae for the rest of his days.

Without breaking stride, the trollkin threw his axe with both hands at the necromancer, all one hundred and twenty pounds of two-headed killing wood and steel, in one mighty overhand toss. From nearly twenty feet away. Like a hatchet. Time seemed to stop for everyone as the five-foot-tall weapon lazily tumbled forward.

"Brak. No!"

Sleipnir had just enough time to realize what the troll-kin had done as the spinning axe connected. The downward-facing blade caught the necromancer in the center of his sternum. The upward-facing blade clipped the staff.

Both failed under the tremendous mass of impact.

The axe split the wizard in half almost as cleanly as it did his magical staff.

For a moment, nothing happened.

Then all the magical energy in both the staff and the wizard was released explosively, a flash of crimson light that blinded the Araneae and nearly caused him to lose his grip on the gray stone bricks.

The whole sky turned red. The moon dripped blood and most stars simply vanished as if day-lit. Afterimages strobed across Sleipnir's eyes.

Bob emerged from the stairway, slightly the worse for wear. Four skeletons had been a bit much, without his two best warriors, but letting that evil bastard sorcerer run loose would have been infinitely worse. He stumbled to a stop. Piper and Princess staggered into him from behind.

The room looked like a polite but clumsy fire elemental had thrown a party. Tapestries were charred and crumbling. Furniture looked cooked. Even leather bindings on books had a scorched appearance. Fresh long-pork assailed his nostrils. Just inside the balcony, he could see Sleipnir keep watch. In the middle of the floor, Brak kneeled next to the badly-burned pieces of the wizard. Tears streamed down Brak's face, carving channels in the ashes.

Brak looked up at Bob with the most mournful eyes he could have ever imagined.

"Woodchuck's dead, Bob," the trollkin said quietly.

Bob blinked, processed, failed, tried again, gave up. "Dead?" He stopped cold in the middle of the room as his legs refused to move any farther. Princess and Piper slid around him on each side and approached their crying companion.

Princess put her hand on Brak's shoulder. "What do you mean dead, honey?" she asked gently.

Brak lifted a roundish blob of black metal the size of his head and held it out to her. Bob could almost smell the heat emanating off of it from where he stood. "Dead."

She stopped and turned a quizzical eye on it. "What's that?"

Sleipnir emerged from his fugue with a shake of the head and took a step into the room, as if willing the shock to wash off his back feet. "That's what happens when a really big flying axe destroys a really bad-ass wizard and his summoning staff. *Boom*." He staggered slightly, even with eight feet to hold him up.

Bob took a step closer, saw the charring around the edges of the Araneae, the singed eyebrows and hair, the ash on his mail shirt. Bob glanced over, realized the front half of Brak was charred as well. Which should have hurt him a lot more, since trolls can quickly heal almost any damage, except acid. And fire. They were especially vulnerable to fire.

He turned back to Sleipnir. "You okay, pal? You look a little cooked."

Sleipnir shook his head again as if to clear it and stared through Bob's head. "Somehow, that axe, Woodchuck, absorbed what just happened. Do you have any idea how much power it takes to melt twelve stones of steel that fast?"

Bob nodded uncomprehendingly, afraid to know that answer. "You're both okay, and the bad guy's dead. That's good enough for me."

"No, it's not," Sleipnir said. He pointed a finger and took a hard step towards Brak's back. "Damn, it, Brak. What did you think you were doing?" he demanded accusingly. Sleipnir took a step, staggered to a stop as Bob stepped in front of him and looked up.

"He was doing what I told him to do, which was stop the guy. At any cost. Okay?"

Sleipnir turned, fought to bring his concentration on the team leader. "Bob, that explosion should have blown the whole top off of this tower and killed all of us." He vibrated with contained energy.

Bob started to say something, but Princess distracted them from their escalating confrontation. "Obviously," she cut them both off sharply, "the gods decided to protect him. And us. Any questions?" She stood in the middle of the floor, with Brak's huge arms wrapped around her waist as the troll-kin cried his eyes out into her stomach. She snarled silently at both of them hard enough that each took a step back in surprise.

Bob looked around, found a none-too-damaged chair, and took a seat. He pulled a wineskin from his pack and tossed it to Sleipnir. "Time for some wine, you think?"

Sleipnir shook his head one last time. "Bob, the gods don't do that. Unless they have something big and nasty planned, you know?"

Bob nodded, exhausted. "Trust me, pal. I'm aware of that."

Bob relaxed with his feet up on the least-damaged foot stool, a glass of the necromancer's good wine in an expensive cut-glass goblet in his hand, wearing a smile. Across the room, Princess continued to console the distraught half-troll as he held the blob of steel in his lap and rocked. Bob shook his head.

Closer by, Piper and Sleipnir worked a variety of low-grade enchanments, mostly Knowings and Divinings, over an amazing collection of small items they had identified as potentially magical. There were books, jewels and jewelry, trinkets, and an ivory wand that was either made from horn of a unicorn or was carved to look like one. Sleipnir was lovingly running his hands over a strangely-shaped sword and murmuring in Elven. Bob watched magical flickers run back and forth between the two.

He took a drink of the excellent wine and leaned forward. "Find something?"

The Araneae, formerly a simple Night Elf who had been turned into a spider centaur creature by his goddess, looked up with new depths of pain in his eyes, as well as greed.

Bob recognized the avarice. It was the same look he saw in the mirror each morning.

Sleipnir took a deep breath and emerged from his concentration. He lifted the blade and cut the air with it to a whistling sound. "This is a Nightblade, Bob. The masterpiece of a Night Elf blademaker."

Bob whistled lightly to himself. "Valuable? Magical?"

The Araneae nodded. "Very. To both. I would like to claim it at part of my share of the treasure."

Bob leaned back, face closed. "If it's that valuable, we'll get it appraised when we get to town and you can made an offer then. For now, Brak needs something."

Sleipnir recoiled as though struck. "Bob, you can't give it to that idiot."

Bob pointed a finger. He saw Piper glance over and shift a bit to free up his hands in case something got out of hand. Even Princess was focused. "That idiot saved your life. And in case you hadn't noticed, Woodchuck's dead. My biggest, toughest, meanest meat shield warrior is unarmed and needs something to fight with. If its magical, all the better."

"Bob," Sleipnir implored, "this is the signature blade of a Night Elf Champion. There has to be something else we can give him."

Bob gave the Araneae a harsh, unbending look. "Then you find me something else he can use, pal, and that blade will get all nicely wrapped up and go on the wagon until we get back to town. Questions?"

Bob watched Sleipnir bite back several comments and take a deep breath. Silently, he nodded to Bob and slid the blade back into an ornate sheath. The centaur rose on all eight spidery feet and looked around the room carefully.

Slowly, Sleipnir walked to a wall and flipped his weight back to climb. Bob stared in awe, as he always did, as the Araneae ascended the wall like it was a floor. The former Night Elf pulled a tapestry off the wall by the shaft holding it up, and dumped the charred fabric on the floor as three pairs of eyes scrutinized. Slowly, he returned to the floor and took his spot next to Bob, holding a ten-foot wooden staff, three inches in diameter, with decorative metal spear-tips at each end.

While everyone but Brak sat rapt, Sleipnir broke off one of the heads and weighed it in his hand.

Bob took a drink of wine and leaned forward. "That won't do it, Sleipnir," he whispered quietly. "It's not nearly enough of a weapon for Brak."

Sleipnir's eyes bored into his, all pain and hunger and anger. "It will be." He lowered his head as if in prayer and magical fires erupted from both hands.

⌁

Bob started from a semi-nap when he heard Sleipnir's voice.

"Bob. It is done."

Bob looked at the results with an eye steeped in years of professional greed. One spear-tip appeared to have been reforged into a single leaf blade for punching, almost like a glaive, black and brown, etched in a way that suggested molten bronze poured into esoteric runes. The other tip was transformed into a scribed cap at the bottom to balance the weight. The ten-foot-shaft now looked coiled, much the same way the unicorn horn was and was scribed much of its length with ancient Elven letters. The room smelled like lightning and charcoal.

Sleipnir and Bob both stood. Bob whistled.

Piper sidled up. "Gods Above and Below, what did you do?"

Sleipnir gave his Puck friend a tired smile. "It is not appropriate for anyone but a Night Elf to bear that blade. I prayed to the dark goddess and asked for her assistance and her blessing."

Princess looked up and hissed at them from where she kept watch over the finally-sleeping half-troll. "On a night when the very gods appear to be involved in our survival? You called on the Dark Mother? You? Are you freaking nuts?"

Sleipnir shrugged. "If they are truly interested, can you think of a better time?"

Piper waved a hand, unleashed a small golden cloud that puffed out larger and thinner around the Araneae and the spear until it silently popped. "Hey, that thing's magical. How did you manage that?"

Bob listened very carefully to the centaur's reply.

"I asked. She answered." Sleipnir took a deep breath, released it. "Princess, can you wake Brak?"

Princess nodded and kneeled down. "Brak, honey, time to get up."

Bob watched wakefulness return to the half-troll, followed by an immense, heavy, sadness. The giant sat up and rubbed his eyes. He picked up the finally-cooled blob of blackened steel and stood to tower over the chest-tall Night Elf woman.

Brak sighed again. "He's gone."

She smiled up at him and put her hand on his arm. "I know, honey, but Sleipnir has something for you."

Brak looked up politely as the Araneae approached, Bob and Piper in his wake.

"Brak, I can't bring back Woodchuck, but I made this for you instead. I know Bob promised to get you a spear when we got back to town, but you needed one now."

Brak took the shaft with reverential awe. "You made this for me? Does it have a name?"

The words seemed to come from nowhere Sleipnir recognized, except from his own mouth. "Its name is *Destiny*."

Bob leaned in and reached up to put a hand on Sleipnir's shoulder and whisper in his ear. "Thank you."

Sleipnir nodded stoically.

⌒

INTERLUDE: BRAK DREAMS

The horizon was an endless, imposing, gray mist, fading to oblivion in the fog.

A beautiful Night Elf woman emerged from the nothingness, elegantly covered in the finest silks, with silvered chain mail armour draped closely across her voluptuous beauty, bearing twinned, crossed Nightblades on her back. Her long raven hair was braided and decorated with a silver and bronze clamp. She approached a giant doorway, the sill and archstone composed of seven great stones, each a different color, as if a rainbow. She knocked lightly with one dainty fist, but the sound seemed to echo across eternity.

The door opened to a giant of a man in furs and heavy armour, a spear in one hand and a horn in the other. He regarded her for a moment with quiet reserved deference.

She drew herself up to her full height, no less giant than the man before her, for all the dream lacked solidity. "Gatekeeper, I seek the Thunderer."

The man nodded once. "He comes."

A second man appeared, even more giant, red hair and beard to his companion's auburn. His furs seemed coarser and more barbaric. His armour was scales worked in copper that suggested a great serpent. His face seemed invisible behind a great beard, all but his piercing blue eyes. In one hand, he bore a silver hammer. "What brings the Queen of the Vanir to this door?"

She nodded regally. "I wish peace between us this night. One of my annoying former servants seeks to play a grand trick on one of your followers. I wish instead to send a boon to your warrior, one that will make him grand and terrible and legendary. Will you grant me your blessing that I may do this thing?"

The Thunderer spoke with a dark voice. "What boon does he seek?"

The Queen of the Vanir smiled. "He seeks the boon of a weapon, to further your cause."

The man considered slowly, while the Gatekeeper stood patiently to one side. "And what would you do, Queen of Ice and Darkness?"

Instead of answering, she cast a blood-red rune into the air between them.

Harsh laughter erupted from both men.

The Thunderer raised his hammer, held it out to her politely. "A prank worthy of the Deceiver. Go in peace, Vanir Queen. Or enter and feast with us as an honored guest this night."

She smiled and crossed the rainbow-colored threshold with a light laughter.

Bob sat calm in the midst of chaos as the team prepared to break camp. On his portable working desk lay his master map of the lost kingdom of Highwynne, stolen from the paladins of *Imperia Sentinalis* and obsessively updated for nearly four years, from Stonemeadow to Estermill to Sagemont. He added the new notes for Fallbourne as he eyed the semi-destroyed wizard's tower from the top of a nearby hill. The place was sealed up tight, magically warded, glamoured over with a few subtle illusions. He considered a few young nobles or interested wizards in Sagemont he could sell the keys to for a very goodly sum of gold. Maybe even enough to let the Araneae buy that sword out of his share. Brak seemed happy with his new spear.

It wasn't Woodchuck. Piper and Princess had both commented to him on the changes that had come over the troll-kin over the last few days, but he seemed to be coming out of his funk. Today, he was like a puppy with a new squeaky toy.

"Bob."

He looked up confused. "Huh?"

Princess towered over him. "I said, 'Get your lazy butt up. We're ready to go.'"

Bob looked around, realized that the whole camp had been cleared, except for his folding chair and portable desk. The mules looked exceptionally put upon, waddling with all the treasure that rat-bastard necromancer had accumulated over decades of evil.

He put away his map, stood, stretched, handed Princes the portable desk, and folded up his chair. "Sleipnir, how quickly straight back to Valland from here?"

The spider-centaur warrior-wizard did a double-take. "I thought we were headed back to Freylake Pass to strip all the gold from Brak's koi pond."

Bob smiled. "I think I'll leave that as a present for Galliarde and the *Imperia Sentinalis* paladins. We've got enough treasure for now."

Princess appeared out of nowhere at his ear. "Piper, has Bob been possessed?"

The Puck was on the case. "Checking." A puff of bright green smoke emerged from his hands and swarmed around Bob like a cloud of gnats. It tickled, too.

"That's not funny, you two." Bob gave them a serious look.

Princess cocked her head at him oddly. "Bob, I've known you for nearly ten years," she said. "I've seen you pry copper nails out of ruined temples to sell for the metal weight. I watched you mug an orc in Dunmerrow for eight copper fennigs and two silver shillings. Of course I think you've been possessed."

Bob scowled at her. "One, we were broke. Two, that orc had it coming. Brak, how do you feel about mugging orcs?"

Brak sauntered up with a smile, Destiny lightly gripped in one hand. "Did you kill him afterwards?" Brak really hated orcs.

"No," Bob said, "Just took his money and his knife."

"Can we go back and finish him off?"

"Brak, honey," Princess interrupted, "that was five years ago. He's moved on by now."

"Oh." Brak had a dejected look. He really, really, really hated orcs.

Bob took half a step back and raised his hands to get everyone's attention. "Is it acceptable if I move on as well?" He got confused looks back. "I mean, we've got a crap ton of gold here. Complaining mules worth. Enough to refit, pick up some better gear." He gave Piper and Sleipnir a greedy look. "Some magical gear? And maybe go after some of the bigger prizes further south. How does that sound?"

Piper watched the cloud dissipate. "Princess, apparently he's not possessed or a doppelganger, after all. This is the real Bob talking." The Puck wizard paused, got a gleam in his eyes. "One other test." He pulled out a silver coin and flipped it in the air.

Bob's right hand shot out like a snake striking and snatched the coin in the air.

Piper nodded to himself. "Yup. That's Bob."

"Okay, that's still not funny."

The rest laughed.

Princess leaned in close. "You feeling well?"

He turned, looked her in the eyes. "Maybe I'm finally growing up."

Bob studied the terrain around them, flat for miles in every direction, save for a small rock outcropping perhaps half a mile ahead. He yelled across the space. "Sleipnir, can we make it in time?" He turned his horse to look back, standing between Brak and Sleipnir, both on foot leading mule trains.

Behind them, a small horde of bandits on horses had appeared on that last ridge. They began to file down the slope at a healthy canter, steadily closing the gap, now only a few miles away.

Sleipnir was the expert on The Wastes. "Probably, if we push right now. But then we're surrounded and trapped."

Bob smiled. "We'll burn that bridge when we get there. Piper, Princess. You drive the mules. Brak, help them, but be ready to fend off a charge. Sleipnir, can you walk backwards fast enough to keep an eye on them?"

The Araneae eyed the terrain with a grimace. "No, but I can keep them off our backs until they get very close. And the first few who try will come home strung over their saddles."

"Good enough," Bob said. "Move."

Even the mules seemed to sense the importance of the situation and picked up the pace rather than resisting. Behind, the pack of marauders slowly closed the distance, willing to run their prey down to the rocks and bottle them up there.

As they closed the last hundred yards to the little stone pile, Bob heard the whoops erupt from behind him over the sound of the horses pounding the dry packed earth. He risked a glance back, saw that the pack appeared to be desert orq riders.

Brak would be pleased to have someone to try his new spear out on, finally.

Ahead, the rocks suddenly loomed before Bob's horse. "Piper, you, Princess, and Sleipnir get up top immediately and make sure nobody else can get up there. Then be ready to kill things down here."

Piper nodded. "What about the horses?"

"I'd rather lose all three horses and walk home than any of the nine mules and all that gold."

Piper smiled as he pulled his little pony to a halt. That sounded like Bob. He looked at the big Araneae scout looming over him. "Let's do this."

Sleipnir smiled. Without breaking stride, he grabbed the Puck wizard around the waist and scampered up the rocks with Princess in close pursuit. The top was small, flat, and generally shear-sided enough that desert brigands would be held at bay for long enough. "Good up here, Bob."

Bob threw himself off his horse, grabbed all the reins and leads, and settled the animals as close to the escarpment as he could, trusting them to stay put like well-trained creatures. He drew his cutlass and slung his shield. This would be over fast enough, one way or the other.

Thundering hooves charged closer. Brak stayed put with his humongous warspear readied. A sudden thwang from Sleipnir's crossbow sounded over the noise, emptied a saddle. Another orq rode close enough to smash a blow into Bob's shield with a clang, took a slash for his efforts that nearly unhorsed him. Brak plunged his spear into the ground, impaling a downed ork like a bug. Two more lay close at his feet, also dead. Panicked horses fled back into the blowing dust. A horn sounded.

Without another word, the orcs retreated to a safe distance, regrouping a hundred yards off. Sleipnir lobbed a sixteen-inch crossbow bolt at their giant leader, saw that monster wave a hand and deflect it while it was still twenty feet away. So. Another sorcerer involved. *This was going to get ugly.*

Bob counted. Seven orqs down around them, all dead. Thirty-odd more over there getting organized for another run. This time, they wouldn't be surprised. *Definitely going to get ugly.*

Brak howled something guttural at them. Over yonder, heads suddenly turned in this direction. Insults were yelled back. Hotheads circled their horses.

Hold on. When had Brak learned orquish?

Bob knew Brak hated orcs more than anything, but had never heard him talk to them. Bob didn't even speak enough of the language to understand the insults flying back and forth. But it sounded pretty insulting.

Brak took three steps forward and shook *Destiny* at them. And apparently said something particularly choice. The leader waved a hand in their direction. Followed by an eldritch bolt that slammed into the half-troll's chest.

Or almost did. It appeared to splash off of a sorcerous shield and spray like water in various directions.

Brak raised his free hand and made a universal gesture in the orcs's direction.

That was apparently enough. They charged.

Bob knew better than to race off and leave the animals alone. "Sleipnir, Princess, Piper. Protect Brak. Now." He settled his shield, his feet, and pulled his hat down to shade his eyes better.

Brak surged forward at a sudden run even as the orqs goaded their own horses into motion. He leveled his greatspear as his long legs shortened the distance quickly. A green blast of energy from Piper struck one rider from his mount. A crossbow bolt went through another. Princess dropped an arrow into someone's shoulder, stealing his attention. And then Brak disappeared into the blowing dust and thundering hooves.

One rider catapulted headlong out of the brown fog, as if his horse had run headlong into a low brick wall. Perhaps one made of troll.

Bob reconsidered the situation. The dust obscured everything more than fifteen feet away. "Everyone get down here right now. We've got to go help him."

Bob lumbered in the direction of the melee, unwilling to run in this heat and this armour, but slower than the other three. They could catch up quickly enough. Princess did first. She drew both blades after she tied a scarf around her lower face. On his other side, Sleipnir moved amazingly sedately, but covered a great deal of ground with his rippled feet. Piper rode standing on his back, one hand on a shoulder and the other ready to cast. Sleipnir had put away his crossbow and drawn his own sword and shield.

As they got close, another ork came flying out of the dust to tumble to a halt at their feet. Princess stopped moving just long enough to stick a poniard in him to make sure. Bob stepped over another body, dead in the dirt with a stove-in chest and entrails eviscerated.

Bob heard Brak's voice ahead of him in the press of horses. He realized that the orqs were actually at a disadvantage now, trying to maneuver themselves around to take a hack at the giant in the swirling, dusty melee.

Sleipnir came up behind a rider and speared him through before the orc even realized they were being attacked from their rear. Bob came upon another and cut a leg nearly off. The dying ork screamed as his arterial blood sprayed into the dirt. Princess leapt in the air over another horse's haunches and landed behind the rider with both blades forward. That one died silently and was pitched to the ground. Bob smiled.

Then they were through the press. The dust parted as the wind died down. On one side, Bob, Princess, Sleipnir, and Piper held a chunk of a large circle. At its center, Brak and the largest spell-casting ogre Bob had ever even heard of, squared off.

Apparently for fun, Sleipnir hauled off and punched the ork nearest him in the jaw, knocking him to the ground unconscious, instead of killing him. The rest of the riders peeled back to face them across the space. Between, the two giants warred.

The ogre held a great sword in one hand while his other glowed with eldritch fire. Bob figured he would need both hands to even lift that weapon, let along swing it. But he also wasn't eight feet tall.

Brak glanced back, saw his friends close. "Stay back. This is honor-combat between Urmonazg and me." He flicked his spear out like a viper's tongue, was blocked by the shield-like spell the ogre wielded.

Urmonazg? Bob felt one of his eyebrows go up involuntarily. This just wasn't like Brak. *Kill them all, then hunt down their cats,* was one of his favorite sayings about orcs.

The orcs, however, kept their own distance, both from the combat and from the newcomers.

Could it get any weirder?

Bob nodded to his companions and settled in to watch, an eye on both groups.. He couldn't do anything about the twenty-odd orcs still vertical without starting a wholesale slaughter, and he wasn't sure who would be the victim at this moment.

Urmonazg, the ogre, raised his left hand and gestured. Purple fire erupted in Brak's direction.

Fire. Not good. But like before, the spectral barrier protected the half-troll, parting the flames like a knife.

Brak growled, surged suddenly forward, and impaled the ogre through the heart before he could react. Urmonazg's eyes bugged out as he looked down in surprise, and then they rolled backwards in his head.

The ogre screamed. It went on and on, the most blood-curdling sound Bob had ever heard. It got higher and fainter until it disappeared like a soap-bubble popping.

Complete silence reigned. Even the horses stood perfectly still.

Brak stood over Urmonazg with his greatspear, *Destiny*, still in the creature's chest. A sudden blue surge of power emanated out of the ogre's chest and flowed up the shaft of the spear. It surged up Brak's hands and seemed to engulf him for the faintest instant.

Bob wasn't sure it wasn't just a trick of the light. He had never seen anything like it.

Brak withdrew his spear from the ogre's chest. Very little blood remained on the blade as Brak pointed it at the orcs in front of him. "Gomoku, Durzum, Karthurg. I own your souls. Return to Lorbank and tell the elders that the north is no longer safe for your kind. I will destroy all who cross the Mihawa River. Hear me and obey."

Bob considered the situation, stood there aghast. It had just gotten weirder.

One of the orcs bowed from horseback, gave Brak a serious look. "It shall be as you command, Dread Lord." Without another word, the ork survivors wheeled their horses and rode back the way they had come, leaving behind the dead half of their company.

Bob flinched at the expression on Brak's face when the giant troll-kin turned his direction. He had seen the man stupid, silly, pained, half-dead, angry, drunk, and completely berserk.

Bob could not remember the thoughtful, serious look Brak had now. His eyes glowed with a fierce blue energy, but it was only for a second, and then his eyes were their normal hazel color.

"Brak, you feeling well?" Bob finally asked.

Brak looked them over, took a deep breath, blinked, and seemed to release some inner demon as he exhaled. "Bob, what just happened?"

Piper cast a small magenta cloud over the entire area. It circled Brak once, and then vanished into the spear-tip with a flash of light. Piper's eyes got huge. "You, uh, kinda, uhm, killed the bad guy, Brak," the Puck wizard stammered.

"Oh." Brak looked around his feet at all the dead orcs, incredulously. "I did all that?"

Bob smiled to calm him. "It would have been worse, but Piper was able to protect you from the ogre's magic."

Piper hopped off Sleipnir's back to sidle up close to Bob and whisper at him as Brak and Princess began stacking bodies to loot. "Bob, I never did anything. Brak was too far away to put any magical protection on him."

"But I saw those spells bounce off him. That ogre should have eaten his lunch."

Piper grimaced. "Bob, that was the spear. Not me."

Bob rounded on Sleipnir. "Just what did you give him?"

Sleipnir's elven face paled completely to white as all the blood drained out and eyes grew to the size of saucers. His mouth was wide enough to catch flies. "I don't know," he whispered back.

the Blacksmith's Song

Chapter 1: The Catacombs

And so the dreams begin anew
  dank dark tunnels
    filled with brackish pools and green light
  cold ugly wind in the storm drains

I knew this place once
  another dream
    another time
  the night that almost never ended

Can you hear the screams echoing?
  they say people lived down here once
    before darkness claimed the sun
  mayhap they are other travelers
    lost to the surface world
a cold and bitter ghost lurks down here
  preying on the lost

In another age
  I fought the master of this place
    a war unlike this world has known
      hordes of ravening beasts
      glittering succubi
    dancing madness
darkness ascendant

That was the time of the Darksong
  rising from these tunnels
    where fell creatures hide
  like the engulfing gray nightfog
come to claim us

Have you never heard that call?
  ringing with ugly greed and callow madness
    his victims live forever in the dark places
  a cold hand on your neck as you pass

I was once his tool
  destroying a world for his pleasure
    and my own foul purpose
  I came with fire and fury
like apocalypse descending

It was a war unlike this world has ever known
  when I turned on him
    and wrought my justice there as well
  like the fires of the blacksmith
and the blows of the hammer

There was left a place
  some call it Carthage now
    but any name will do
  for only the ruins remain
and they tell no tales

There are only the tunnels below
  still festering with the darksong
    a cold ugly place
      where angels never tread

It is a war never-ending
  fought now in his domain
    with fire and salt
  blood and fury
and the angel's dream

Between us
  in the wan green light
    all his creatures stand
  quivering with the fear of our wrath

No laughter or prayers can touch him here
  safe in the folds of the darksong
    he smiles wicked and proud
  knowing he can be savaged here
but never truly defeated

That darkness can never be felled
  never quieted
    never quenched
  for it lurks in every heart
singing quietly

But I have not come on the path of righteousness
  no angel's dream guides me
    mine is the mission of vengeance
  I will be content to slay him without
because I can master him within

In a blink he knows to fear
  for he is immune to the white fire
    but no angel's hand has touched my blade
  it still glows red with the Blacksmith's Song
seeking a heart to quench the flames

My smile no less evil than his was
  just a second ago
around me those arrayed hordes quail
  clamoring to flee their trap reversed
    there are screams of terror and the Blacksmith's Song

It was a war unlike this world had ever known
  darksong waxing and waning across horizons
    content to corrupt those innocent souls
Until I learned the Blacksmith's Song
  his blade lighting the tunnels a terrible red glow
    swallowing the green light

There was a truce for a time
  but he broke it in his greed
    looking to visit me his wrath
Can you hear the screams from the tunnels?
  one of those lost souls was a seer once
the dragon awakened instead
  and now I bring vengeance to this place

The dreams begin anew
  dank dark tunnels
    filled with brackish pools and green light
  and that cold ugly wind in the storm drains

He has shown me the path
  and awakened the last Carthaginian
    those cries of madness give way to terror
  as my footsteps approach
for it will be a war unlike this world has ever known

Chapter 2: the City

In the cry of a nightbird
  I heard an echo of her voice
    it took me back to another age

We stood together
  arms entwined and hearts racing
    looking down from a balcony
  as the Festival crowds danced below
    somewhere in the stars and laughter and her eyes
      the magic was born

It was the birth of summer in the rites
  ripening fields of grain lined the roads
    orchards grew heavy and fat
  and our love blossomed as well

We had but a few summer months together
  before a shadow crossed her heart
    I felt the cold of death in her touch
      and heard mocking laughter from the night

Have you ever heard of the Wars?
  I sought out the master of darkness
    and found him already safe in my home
  laughing

In my last memory of the city
  seen from that ridge north of the river
    it was still burning in places
  looted clean in others
ground into the soil and salted as well

In fighting the minions of darkness
  I had become one myself
    wreathed in fire and the steelsong

putting to torch and blade all I had known
for the betrayal I had faced
in the form of a brother

He escaped retribution
and still hides in his master's shadow
together beneath the ruins of that city

In the years since that day
I have crossed worlds and dreams
first there was Mountain
standing high and unpassable athwart my road
grinding down all who might surrender to despair
and surrendering
to those who would sacrifice yesterday for tomorrow

later I was a revenant in the Desert
beneath a killing hot sun
surrounded by the sands
watching them slowly claim my lost home
while I healed a fractured heart and soul

and then there was Sea
a blue desert and the mountain known as winterstone
no less deadly than the past
in crossing it I lost everything again
shattered on an unknown beach

I heard her voice
in the call of a nightbird
she is still quietly crying

Chapter 3: Stonedancer Vision

For eight nights I had the dream
  calling my name from behind closed eyes
    tonight is no different

I saw a land of darkness to infinity
  lit by falling stars
    dying songs

Each light that fell was gone
  silver flashing to crimson
    and then nothing
  each day the darkness grew

I passed through this realm
  lost and alone
    where even angels fear to tread
  beyond both hope and despair

There the dream always ended
  but tonight it draws me deeper instead

At first the sound is without meaning
  then it becomes a distant mountain's heartbeat
    it might be an ancient engine
    such an image is in my memory

Closer now it grows
  leading me to a soft red glow
    a cave overlooking my unmarked road
  the ringing sound engulfs me
taking me down to the heart of a mountain

With no wind to blind me
  I suddenly realize
    how cold the night had become
    cutting through me

But here I can feel the mountain's heat
  leeching the cold from my bones
    with the red stone warmth

A thousand miles down I find a cathedral
  lit by the fireglow of the flowing lava
    the ringing sound deafens me
  but the origin is clear now

Legends speak of the Blacksmith
  living outside the angel's fire and the darksong
    answering to no power save his own

Here in the heart of a mountain
  I watch a sword take shape in his hands
    his anvil like an altar in this stonemight cathedral
    red steel singing under his hammer

For an eternity I stand there
  bound within the sound of the stonemight
    lines of power pulse in the stone
      answering his call

There was silence as sudden as death
  the song ended
    and hung echoing into this vast cathedral
  as he looked up at me

His eyes were silverfire aglow
  the magic that had brought me here drew me in further
    for a moment we joined

His heat flowed into my limbs
  rivers of power flowing from the stonemight
    and I saw the road

The vision ended as the song did
  I opened my eyes to darkness
    a void a deep as the darksong

Nine steps brought me to the anvil
  on it I found the sword
    waiting as if it were an altar instead

The metal was cold until I touched it
  and then a red steel glow began
    lighting the cavern a pale memory

I heard the Earthmother whisper the name stonedancer
  and I saw that road again
    bounded by mountains and lit red

Beyond the mountains there was desert
  beyond desert awaited ocean
    beyond water there were mountains again
it was the red road before me

Chapter 4: Earthmother

She came down from the wilderness
  seeking warriors for the apocalypse
    men to fight and die for her dream
her call brought me thus

In another age
  I might have remained a scholar
    but there was no ignoring her call

It was like that night
  so many years ago
    when the Blacksmith first came for me
  riding from that same wilderness

In a dream I heard her voice
  a call whispered on the night breezes
    calling my name among many
  but each name I recognized
    each phase of my existence has brought a new name
  she called them one by one

The final name was one I knew not
  until I heard her call

She brought me to this valley
  her stonemight cathedral in the wilderness
    standing alone in the first light of dawn
    Warrior

The names called to the morning
  rang like words of power off the trees
    answered by the beast of darkness

Though many times my war has known her cause
    this is the first
    when I have fought under her banner

but I have been the Blacksmith's sword for so long
  I no longer question my fate

It is enough that I fight the Master of Darkness
  cloaked in the red light of vengeance
    existing in the balance between angel's fire and darksong

The battle joined is like any other
  in a lifetime of war
    covering most of the world
    and all of eternity

Once I was of the Lost
  proud warriors gone beyond the edge of the world
    and nearly forgotten

In our youth and arrogance
  we fought to the heart of the darksong
    seeking to break his hold
    wielding the might of the angel's fire

One by one my brothers fell
  twisted by the dark one to his foul purpose
    through night we fought
    but only I stood unbroken
      when dawn crossed our ruins

I tried to return home
  only to find the darkness already resident
    so I burned that place to ruins as well
    and turned in despair back to the wilderness

In a red cathedral I found the answer
  in a vision of the Blacksmith
    slowly forging a sword of many names
    icons like totems down the blade
      and I was each of them

With his purpose fused into my soul
  I returned to the wilderness
    wandering as before
     but the Earthmother called
    seeking warriors for the apocalypse
  men to fight and die for her dream
calling my name in dream and midnight whisper

Chapter 5: Cathedral

My cathedral was the sky
  a symphony as grand as the wilderness
    ringing through the rocks and trees
      with the unquenchable fury of an avalanche

The mountains stood sentinel
  pulsing with the gathered power
    trees swayed and limbs snapped taut
      the first screams started in the canopy

Off in the distance I heard her song begin
  mysterious harmony
    and yet as familiar as my heartbeat
  a ringing counterpoint to the distant thunder

For another moment I felt it rise
  and then the song engulfed me
a baptism by song
  followed quickly by the driving rain

I have known torture less painful
  than the beauty of her song
    gathering me within its folds
      closer and closer to that whirling center

My cathedral had been the sky
  and the altar was now a towering anvil
    reaching from mountain to stars
      an eerie calm settling in its shadow

But for the grace of her song
  I would be lost now
    hammered down by that monster
  ground out like an ant

Even now I feel her caress
  a glowing nimbus of power
    coming between me and the storm
    as the song drags me forward

I remember daylight
  it was just failing when she found me
    the darkness is growing thick and cold
    but still her song rings

On the mountaintop a flash of silverfire
  like a lightning bolt held stable
    from within it her voice
    calling the storm to her

Can you hear the call of the stormsinger?
  Stormlady moon to the wayward sons
    lover and protector on the widepath
    calling me like a mighty war-horn

My cathedral was the sky
  a symphony as grand as the wilderness
    ringing through the rocks and trees
    with the unquenchable fury of an avalanche

Like so many of the characters I write, Jesilyria's story presented here is part of a much larger story arc. We do not exist for a few days and then Happily Ever After. Instead, there are struggles, and little victories, and adventures. There is an entire world to discover beneath the Spine of the Giants, and I hope you will enjoy this first tidbit about the dragon.

Falling into the Dragon's Spine
Part 1: Hope

Jesilyria paused as Ylwa perked up from her spot beside the small fire. The big sheepdog carefully sniffed the chilly breeze, her ears forward, tail straight out. Just as Jesilyria was about to reach for her loaded staffbolt, Ylwa whined happily and began to wag her tail. Jesilyria looked around at the area around her small campsite, counted sixteen sheep in immediate sight and knew the other seven were either within Ywla's scent range, or her sight. The she-hound was smart enough to handle the job herself. Jesilyria was mostly along to get the stupid ruminants out of trouble when Ylwa couldn't. It made her life a little easier. Not easy. Just, not as hard.

Nissa came around a corner of the trees and spied her, a laden leather backpack on her back. "Why do you always come up here? Can't you find the sheep grass down closer to the village?"

Jesilyria shrugged. She always did when Nissa asked. It verged on ritual now. She checked the small pot of oil warming on the fire, but it was still several minutes from boiling, so she shifted it slightly to just keep it warm.

Nissa got thoroughly sniffed and inspected by Ylwa before she drew up a spot on a downed log across the fire. Ylwa shifted around and stretched out so she could keep everyone in sight and still get an itchy ear attended to.

Jesilyria considered her closest friend as Nissa began pulling small bundles from the backpack, comparing herself to her so-diametrically-opposite friend. Herself a tiny blond waif who could pass for younger than her fourteen years. Nissa so much more developed that she was often mistaken for an older girl. Herself spare and lean to Nissa's lush brunette bumps and curves. So few words, when Nissa nattered nonchalantly, continuously. Her own quiet dreams compared to Nissa's grand visions for her future.

Jesilyria shrugged again. "Better fodder. Fewer people."

Nissa unwrapped a wedge of cheese and broke off a piece for a politely attentive Ylwa. Tail wagging ensued. Nissa studied her closer than normal for a beat. "Jes, I'd like to say you haven't been the same since your father died, but you were like this then, too. Maybe you're just more open about it now."

Jesilyria shrugged a third time. It got to be a habit around Nissa. "Plague's plague. Someone has to watch the sheep. It's quiet here."

Nissa eyed her knowingly with a smile. "And nobody is around to bother you when you dream your weird dreams.

Jesilyria started to shrug, nodded instead. "I don't like people."

Nissa unwrapped a sausage and pulled a knife to cut slices. She smiled saucily. "They aren't all bad. In fact, some of the village boys can be quite—"

Jesilyria looked up, her tone sharper than she expected. "You haven't...?"

Nissa winked at her. "No, silly. One must remain pure for First Night, in order to please the Herttua. Our Lord would be quite angry. But there are things you can do and still remain pure." An unconscious tongue slipped out and wet her lips at the memory.

Jesilyria blinked in surprise and lapsed back into silence. A few slices of sausage extended the gap in conversation. For a moment, she considered what it would be like to be an object of some boy's desire. She remembered how her parents had been, Isä coming in from the fields and grabbing Äiti as she cooked, the groping, the kissing, the giggling.

But, First Night. That day, seventeen months hence, when she turned sixteen years old and would be taken up to the castle, to be made woman by the Duke. Would she then be married off to some village boy if she pleased the Duke, expected to bear many children in the wake of the plague and hard living? Or worse, become a second or third wife to one of the wealthier men? A brood ewe? A gimmer?

No. Not for her. Not for some man to tell her what she could do. Not when there was so much more out there in the world to see.

One hand closed on the little metal charm her mother had given her, pinned to her breast and intended to ward off evil. Äiti even claimed it was enchanted with a woman's magic, but that wouldn't protect her that night. That wasn't evil. *Was it?* Just the unacceptable way of things.

No.

Nissa eyed her close, probably read her mind. That wouldn't be hard to do. Nissa smiled. "It won't be the end of the world, Jesi."

Jesilyria struggled to find the words. "Yes, it will."

Nissa gnawed on some cheese and took a swig of well-watered wine from a skin. "Why?"

Jesilyria considered it. "Because I want more."

Nissa gave her a sudden sad look, decades beyond her years. "You won't get it, Jes."

Jesilyria watched Nissa silently inventory the well-tended camp. The pot of warm oil mixed with berry juice. The wood branches and logs shaped into molds for the boiled leather. The tiny metal anvil where she could peen rivets when leather-working. By her foot, the quiver where she kept a brace of spare missiles for the staffbolt. Tucked into her own backpack, the cloth roll where she stored her father's tools.

Jesilyria felt the sting deep in her stomach. "I have to try."

Nissa nodded sagely. "I know. I brought you something."

She rooted around the bottom of her pack as Ywla watched, nose intent on more treats. Nissa pulled a cloth-wrapped bundle and handed it across the fire. "Aatto the cobbler sent these and asked if there was anything else you needed. Apparently, three rabbits freshly skinned made a pretty pair of house slippers for someone and he was very well paid."

Jesilyria caught her breath and bit her bottom lip as she took the heavy weight in her hands. She unwrapped bundle and pulled out a tiny pair of boots in very dark brown, rich with a rubbed smell of lanolin. They were much heavier than the soft boots she wore now, several layers thick with a hardened shell and thick soles inset with metal studs to keep traction on snow and ice. She tapped the toes and heard a rewarding metal thunk under a layer of leather.

Jesilyria remembered to breathe. She looked up to see Nissa smiling down at her. "If that's the last piece, I want to see the whole thing. Especially after all the odd things you've had me trade to people to get the bits and pieces you need and then haul it all the way up here where no one can see it."

Jesilyria panicked for a moment the thought, at revealing herself, even to her best friend. One hand trailed unconsciously to the small wooden box she was sitting on, covered with sheepskin to keep the her butt warm and the wood dry. Her heart stuttered, like running down a steep shale embankment. The box was something her father had stored sweaters in during the summer, pine veneered with cedar. Before. Something she had claimed when her mother unraveled the old sweaters to make things for her and her little brother, Jaska. Something hers.

Nissa leaned close. "Please?"

Jesilyria wavered. This was her Hope Chest. Not like the one her mother kept for when she was married, filled with lacey and frippery. Pretty, and girlie, and grown-up. Those were her mother's hopes. She patted the box. Here were hers. It was filled with pretty and practical, but not the kind her mother would understand.

Jesilyria was a different kind of practical.

But this was Nissa. This was the friend who had been with her through the best and the worst. Who listened to her dreams, even when they didn't make any sense. Who kept her secrets safe. Who traded with the smith, and the cobbler, and Iikka the cattle herder for her, bringing her the little prizes that made it worth coming out here and spending days on end camped and watching over stupid sheep. Nissa, the chatterbox who had never told a soul. Nissa.

Jesilyria swallowed a dry mouth, felt her heart climb back down out of her throat. "Okay."

Slowly she stood up and unlatched the box.

Part 2: Fashion

Nissa remembered to close her mouth, after it fell open a third time. Words failed her. Paragraphs failed her. Coherent thought largely failed her, although that happened frequently anyway and she rarely let it interrupt the stream of words coming out of her mouth. Not that the boys were ever listening anyway, other than to pay attention when she breathed. She did that well. They appreciated it ever more. Heaving bosoms covered many social faux pas. When done right, anyway. She practiced that regularly.

Now, silence.

Jesi stood there, anxious, fragile, exposed, waiting for her words. And they failed her. "Wow."

She watched Jesi's face take on an even-more-anxious cast. "That's it?"

Nissa nodded. She recovered her vocabulary, somewhat, and discovered the word she needed. "Awed."

"Odd?"

Nissa shook her head. "No. Awed. In awe. Jesi, that's simply amazingly wonderful. Wow. That you could do all that. I had no idea you were that good."

She watched Jesi look down and take her own inventory. "Really?"

Nissa nodded. Silent. Awed. "Wow. No, turn around slowly so I can see it all."

Nissa applied the critical eye that would make her a very successful First Wife soon. Fashion. Drape. Color. Line. Bias. Silhouette.

The boots she knew. Heavy. A man's style, like both of their fathers wore daily for muck, mire, and rocks. But petite, for the waif who demanded more out of life.

Over the boots, a pair of boiled, hardened, leather pieces protecting the front and sides, and running from her ankle to just above her bent knee. Jesi called them *greaves* and patterned them after one of the images in a book she had acquired when this strange dream descended on her a year ago.

Like all the cow's leather, this was a deep indigo-maroon color, one they had experimented with by mixing summer berries into the oil when they boiled the leather. It was rich, but subtle, almost the color of the sky just when the light faded at sunset. It made Jesi's blue eyes and pale blond hair snap in a way that would bring the boys running, if she ever developed an interest in that sort of thing.

Jesi's usual leggings were made from lined sheepskin, durable and warm on cool summer days, and a wonderfully snuggly inner layer when the snows came, if you had to get out of bed. Over that, a tough pair of knee-length leather britches made from one of Iikka's hides, regularly riveted with rectangular pieces of long-boiled leather tougher than wood, and laced in front.

At her waist hung a twirly skirt made up of strips of semi-hardened leather, again riveted with several pieces of harder leather, what her book called *brigandine*. The strips were a hand wide each, and there was a second layer underneath, offset by two fingers. It wouldn't twirl much, being only to mid-thigh, and would be positively immoral without several layers and pants underneath. Plus, Jes was not the kind of girl who would twirl with it. Nissa considered making her own kilt for summer. She knew twirly.

Jesi had protected her middle with a pretty girdle, a belt made of square leather pieces the size of her palm, riveted together once along the middle of the flat sides so she would have the most flexibility. Then she had peened several more rivets around the edges to make it tougher. Nissa had one just like it at home that she had shown to Jesi, although hers was made purely to draw the eye to her tucked in waist and show off her lush curves. Jesi really didn't have any curves to show off.

Over her sheepskin inner tunic, Jes wore a tougher leather tunic, dyed a lighter shade than everything else because it hadn't been in the oil long enough to make it rigid. But it made a nice contrast, closer to red than indigo. Nissa approved of the color combination, especially on Jesi. Her own coloring looked better in paler shades and greens, but friends needed to look out for each other, especially in fashion.

It wasn't like Jesilyria had any fashion sense at all.

The tunic had been laced at the sides, Nissa understood, to keep the material intact and tough across the belly. Not that she could envision getting into a fight where someone would want to cut her. But she also didn't dream of life beyond the mountains. Her eyes kept traveling up her friend's spare frame.

Jesi had fashioned an extra-rigid piece of hardened leather for her upper chest laminated with several other pieces riveted on. A man would call it a breastplate, but it only came down to her shoulder blades in back and only barely past her sternum in front, connected at the top of her shoulders by straps riveted in.

Shoulder pieces, what Jesi called *pauldrens*, covered the points and were attached to other pieces coming down her arms like snake scales and laced underneath. The whole thing was a clamshell, laced up the sides.

Very practical.

Nissa had put her foot down here, however, demanding that Jesi shape the front to include a much larger bosom the Jesilyria had, for many reasons. She might suddenly develop breasts, although her mother was barely larger. She could always add padding underneath to protect herself in combat. The curves would cause a man to pay more attention to her chest than her eyes anyway.

And didn't every woman want to have an impressive bosom, especially when facing a strange and hostile world? Isn't that why the gods made women's breasts so nice? To keep men distracted?

Jesi had refused, however, to peen little rivet flowers where her nipples would appear on the enhanced bust. That was a pity. Men would get positively stupid around her then. Easily swayed. More easily swayed. Nissa suppressed a sigh over lost arguments. This was too important to Jesi.

Another piece of hardened leather wrapped around Jesi's neck and collarbones, providing protection without limiting her movement and laced up the front. Seams were always important, but especially so when making armor. It had to work, but so few men understood that it had to look good as well. Men.

Jesi's forearms were protected by semi-rigid tubes of leather, clamshelled together, laced, and peened into a decorative swirly shape. Nissa approved of the bracers and considered asking Jesi to make her some for summer. She was really gifted at leather working. Perhaps that would be enough to keep her in the village, afterwards. One could dream, couldn't they?

Jesi locked eyes with Nissa. "Ready?"

Nissa nodded, silent, afraid to break the spell that had come over her friend when she began to don the armor. This was someone else entirely. She watched Jes turn and bend over to pull the last piece out of her hope chest. That's when she noticed a new addition to the armor, something Jesi hadn't ever mentioned before. She would have remembered that. "What's that?"

Jesi glanced back over her shoulder with a wry grin and an innocent mien. "What's what?"

Nissa pointed. "When did you add a tail?"

Jesi shocked her utterly by wiggling her butt in a most girlie fashion. Nissa would have bet she couldn't have done that without falling over. It took practice. Especially to do it right. She knew.

Twelve pieced of leather had been shaped and peened together like a tail, decreasing in size as they went until the last, oversized, piece, which was shaped like an arrowhead. Like everything else, the tail was indigo maroon. A sudden hip wiggle caused the tail to snap out to one side, taking Nissa's eyes with it. She fought to focus back on Jesi, suddenly understanding why a tail had been added. It provided the same sort of protection from the back as the oversized breastplate did from the front. Distraction.

Jesi smiled slightly and bit her lip. "It goes with the helmet."

Nissa digested that impish tidbit carefully, unsure who this new person was and what had happened to the timid little field mouse sitting here just a short time ago. Words failed her, again. Helmet? "Oh?"

She watched her friend pull a final something from the chest and turn to face her. Jesi's hands covered things up such that she couldn't see clearly, beyond the indigo maroon leather pattern from before, mixed with something else. Then it went atop her head, got strapped down, and the hands came down.

Yes, indeed. A helmet. On the one hand, very practical. Jes was a very practical girl. This would cover her head nicely, protecting against rain and wind, most assuredly insulated for cold and waterproofed with fresh lanolin. She did those things. And the horns were probably practical, as well, being that they looked like someone had cut apart the hardest parts of a ram's skull to form the top of the helmet, and left the horns attached to protect the sides of her head and parts of the rear. After all, that's what they did on the idiot ram whose horns these had been. The whole thing was stitched together with peened leather in an agreeable pattern.

But the snout was just too much.

Nissa finally had to stand and walk around Jesi to get the whole effect. Yes, it was a snout. Made from leather, shaped and layered with brigandine pieces that looked like scales. Just like the rest of the helmet. Nissa glanced down, saw the tail again. Of course. Tail. Helmet. Snout. She took three steps back and saw the dragon now. And Jesilyria had disappeared into the dragon. Nissa nodded. "So no one can see your face."

Jesi's anxious smile turned impish again. "Exactly. I'm not little Jesi who is so much smaller and weaker than all the other kids. Now I'm a big scary maroon dragon."

Nissa cocked her head to digest the whole outfit again. Who was this armored beast? And what had happened to Jes? "I'm surprised you didn't add something to breath smoke and fire out."

Jesi mumbled something.

Nissa leaned closer. "What was that?"

Jesi heaved a put-upon sigh. "I couldn't get it to work."

Nissa goggled, jaw agape, then stopped and thought for a moment. "Let me ask someone in the village. I have an idea. How much longer will you be camped up here before you drive them back down to the village?"

Jesi shrugged, pulled the helmet off, and turned back into a shy, quiet fourteen year old girl. "You brought me sausage and cheese. I have enough meal and flatcakes to stay up here another three or four days if the weather stays nice."

Part 3: Sheep

Jesilyria watched Nissa as her friend disappeared around the bend. She'd done it. She had really pulled it off.

Nissa, who had known her forever, had looked at her in a whole new light. Jesi was something more than just that quiet, strange girl that none of the boys looked at and who wasn't interested in the mundane things the village girls wanted to talk about. Nissa had listened to her dream and not laughed. And now, she had looked at the Dragon in shock. Good shock. Surprised shock. "Wow, you did that?" shock. Jesilyria grinned so hard her face hurt.

Ylwa looked at her like she had lost her mind, but she always did that. She was a dog.

Jesilyria put her armor away carefully and thought about breathing fire. It was a fun thought. She walked around and counted sheep.

Maybe they counted her. They were sheep.

She looked at the afternoon sky and decided that Nissa was likely to get wet before she got home. It had that feel to it. Kinda gray and orange and rainy and windy coming. Good time to pack things up and move them into the rough overhang of rock she used as a shelter when it rained or snowed. The night looked wet and nasty

Under Ylwa's supervision, the sheep were rounded up and moved under the overhang as well. They complained. It did them no good. They were sheep. Ylwa was having none of it. She watched as Jesilyria stretched a few leg-width downed trees across the opening to keep them tucked in and then plopped down in front and only had to growl occasionally when one of them decided to get close. Sheep were dumb.

Jesilyria and Ylwa settled in front of the built-up fire, ate their dinner, and watched the light fade behind the clouds as the wind rose to a chilled howl. The rains followed soon after, driven hard by the long-flat western plains on the other side of the mountains. Jesilyria had never been to the other side of the Spine Of The Giants, but she remembered her father talking about traveling for weeks across flat, wet lowlands to get to the western sea when he was a young merchant. Just grass that ran forever. Nothing to block the wind until it hit the Spine head on. At least on the eastern slopes it had tamed somewhat, after bouncing into the air.

She lived in the lee of things.

They all did, but she wanted to see the western sea. The river to the east ran north, cold and sluggish until it ran into the northern sea, frozen most of the year anyway. Only seal hunters and pirates lived up there anyway. But the west had people. She would meet them.

Jesilyria smiled as she fell asleep to the screaming winds. It sounded like a beckoning song.

The morning woke cold and hollow. Gray skies hung solid overhead, but the winds had died. The world felt frozen, but the air was actually kinda warm. Jesilyria tasted it with her tongue. Poised, perhaps. Like she was. Just out of reach.

Ylwa escorted the bleating sheep out of the shelter and across the nearby vale. There were downed limbs everywhere, but the wind had actually blown away snow in a few places, revealing green treats to hungry lambs.

Jesilyria looked around and decided that the day needed the Dragon. It was who she was going to be. She needed to get used to it.

At least where no one was around to laugh at her. She was alone, with sheep. Ylwa would keep her secrets.

Jesilyria returned to the shelter and geared up for battle with whatever hordes of evil minions fate decided to throw at her today.

She transferred her mother's charm from her regular jacket to the sleeve of her new armour, tied into the laces holding the left shoulder in place. And she had the loaded staffbolt if she needed to shoot anything. Not that there was anything to shoot at beyond the muddy hillside she normally practiced her archery on.

The Dragon emerged to the frantic barking of a frantic sheepdog. She checked the staffbolt, grabbed her quiver and sprinted out of the notch and around the crown of the hill. Combat was at hand.

Wait? Combat? What do I do? Listen to Ylwa. She knows.

The sound led Jesilyria to a stony clearing. It was just the sort of place sheep never went, so of course they had. Stupid sheep.

Jesilyria stopped to take in the scene. Strange smells in the air. Dry and sepulchral. Wet and earthy. Frantic dog.

The storm had knocked down a gigantic old tree. Ripped the roots right up and toppled it over. Fortunately, away from her campsite clearing. And had slammed it into the side of a little rise, cracking the hillside like an egg to reveal a hollow spot inside. The top of the tree disappeared into the hole like an bolt into a winter squash.

Ylwa stood beside the tree and barked one last time as Jesilyria scampered up, staffbolt pointed forward, safety off. The she-hound grew silent and gave her a look.

Jesilyria paused to control her breath. She heard a quiet bleat coming from the hole. Stupid sheep. She knew better than to ask how or why the sheep had climbed atop the trunk and gotten in where it couldn't get out. They were sheep. It was why nobody needed to herd mountain goats. Nothing else in the world was as stupid as a hungry sheep.

Jesilyria rubbed Ylwa behind the ear. "Good job."

There was nothing to it but to try to get the stupid ruminant out. She raced back to camp to grab her gear, stuffing useful things into a backpack against need.

Jesilyria returned and inched her way carefully ono the trunk, using her staffbolt as a balance. She took a length of rope from the pack and tied it to the exposed roots. That way she could at least get herself back out.

Carefully, she crab-walked down the wet bark. It was rough and firm as ground, like walking down an incline. She stopped, thought about it, and decided she could do this without going to the village to get Nissa to bring some boys out. They would tease her about it forever. And then want to come out and look in this hole. And maybe never leave. Stupid boys.

At the entrance, Jesilyria ducked a little and slipped into the hole.

On the other side, enough morning light came in that she could see clearly. The trunk had been stripped of branches in breaking through, leaving a mess of shattered wood and leaves everywhere. The ceiling was twenty feet tall, and the walls looked to be made of cast bricks mortared together in places, and polished carved stone in others.

The idiot sheep had hopped off a branch to get at the leaves, and couldn't get back up again. It stood there chewing noisily, looking about as smart and content as a sheep got.

Jesilyria climbed off the trunk and stood behind the sheep.

It chewed.

She took a deep breath verging on a sigh. She looked around, lay down her staffbolt, and bodily lifted the creature under the belly until it could stand on the trunk. It looked at her placidly, as sheep do, until she grabbed the staffbolt and chivied it up the trunk. The sheep ambled up the trunk and exited at the top.

Jesilyria caught her breath and thought mean thoughts about fresh mutton. Stupid sheep. "A thank you would be nice."

No answer. Just as well. They were sheep.

She was just about to climb out herself when she saw a flash of light. Jesilyria stopped, looked hard into the darkness, and pointed her staffbolt downrange, just in case.

You never knew. Of course, whatever it was hadn't eaten the stupid sheep.

She let her eyes adjust to the darkness.

Something was there. And the darkness seemed to go on behind it. Her eyes got sharper.

Jesilyria could make out a figure. It looked human. It didn't move, but there was a glow that seemed to emanate from it. She took a step, staffbolt centered, safety off, ready to shoot.

She glanced down to find her footing and realized that her mother's charm was glowing very faintly, a soft baby blue that mimicked the glow from over there.

What was it doing? What was it supposed to do?

Her mother had always said that the charm would protect her against bad things, but never specified what. And it wasn't the sort of thing a grown-up fourteen-year-old would ask.

Maybe that was a mistake. Easy enough to fix. Perhaps, just perhaps, her mom had something useful to contribute to the conversation after all. Maybe.

Jesilyria bit her lip and took another step closer, eyes on the glow over there.

It got a little brighter. Enough to show a man seated on the cold stone floor. A dead man.

She took another step.

Very, very dead.

A sudden sound behind Jesilyria nearly made her wet her pants as she jumped off the floor. She spun around, but it was just Ylwa, standing on the trunk and looking in the hole.

Ylwa whined quietly a second time.

Jesilyria took a couple of deep breaths to calm her heart and settle the stomach back down in her guts. "Stay."

Ylwa cocked her head sideways, that "you're an idiot, are you sure about this?" look she got from the big sheep-dog frequently. Usually correctly.

Jesilyria nodded and made a shooing motion with one hand. "Yeah, I know. Go watch the sheep. I'll be along."

Ylwa gave her one more look, and then carefully backed out of the opening and barked a few times to start rounding up the stupid sheep.

Jesilyria swallowed against a dry mouth, pushed her heart back down her throat. She turned to the dead guy. Yes. Still dead. Still glowing. She took another step.

The ceiling was easily sixteen feet in this tunnel. Smooth floors under the broken branches and leaves. Twelve feet wide. Polished. Man-made, although men didn't work on this scale. She paused, gasped, stopped, one foot poised short of another step.

Giants. This hill was part of the range known as The Spine Of The Giants, because on a map, that's exactly what it looked like. A spine.

This tunnel was giant-size.

But that was a man. Human. Nearly two heads taller than her, she guessed from over here, but only two. Not twelve or thirteen feet tall. Six.

Jesilyria remembered to breath. She put her foot down, balanced, and took another step. The glows seemed brighter, both from her charm and from the man. Another step.

She was close enough now to reach out with the staffbolt and poke the figure. Not that she planned to.

The light was as bright as a good tallow candle now. She could read by it if she'd brought a book down here.

He was definitely dead. Dried fruit left out all summer on a rock dead.

The glow came from his lap. She moved a little closer. He was holding a really long knife in his hands. There was a stone in the pommel bigger around than two of her fingers. It glowed. The pommel looked like gold. The blade looked shimmery, without a fleck of rust on it. Which was weird, since his armor had dry-rotted in place just as much as he had. Little dribbles of rust marked empty spots where the armor studs in the leather had corroded to nothing. His beard had deteriorated to just a few wisps of hair. The eyes were closed and shriveled.

Jesilyria thought about it, and decided she'd heard too many ghost stories. She prodded the corpse in the middle of his chest with her staffbolt, primed to fire. It kind of crumbled inward where she pressed. She screwed up her courage tighter and pushed at him from the side. He sort of came apart as he fell over.

She felt kinda bad about that, but decided that it was a good thing. No undead monsters showing up in her dreams to chase her down and eat her.

No new ones.

She let go the breath she had forgotten she was holding. Her heart started to slow down to only beating crazy fast. She rocked back onto her heels again. Relax.

Jesilyria leaned the staffbolt against the wall and kneeled down beside the dead warrior. The short little sword had fallen out of his hands. She picked it up and the glow from it and her charm vanished, dropping her into darkness so deep as to be solid. She squeaked and scrambled backwards on her butt, dropping the poniard back onto the corpse as she did.

After a few seconds, the light returned, hesitantly at first, but building strength. Her charm lit up as well. The corpse sat perfectly still.

Jesilyria pulled her backpack off and flipped it open. She retrieved and unwrapped a small brass lantern that had belonged to her grandfather. She checked it for cracks, filled the reservoir from a small flask, and built a small pile of kindling, looking up and around every three seconds. It was slow going.

Eventually, she got the lantern lit. The sword still glowed. Her charm answered it.

She moved closer, lantern in her left hand, and reached out with her right. She plucked the longknife up and held it firmly. Sure enough, the light went out. So did her charm. The lantern stayed lit.

Weird.

No, worse.

Magic.

Jesilyria studied the blade. For him, it was probably a long knife. For her, almost a sword. A grip large enough for a big man to hold comfortably. Eighteen inches of blade, two inches wide at the guard, tapering down to a sharp point, edged down both sides to within an inch of the crossguard. The blade shimmered in the lantern light, almost like water held solid in her hands. It was marked with what looked like runes down both sides as well. Perhaps a word, but she didn't know the language

Very weird. And it should have been rusted. But the glow had meant it was magical.

Magical?

The charm glowing meant it was magical, too, didn't it? What else was magical?

Jesilyria rocked back on her heels.

What else *was* magical? Was her mother an enchantress? Were others in the village? The Duke? Hadn't he been Duke forever? Was there really magic in the world, just waiting to be found?

Chasms opened in her mind where sturdy walls had once stood.

Crap.

Jesilyria pulled out her waterskin and drank it half down, suddenly dry with apprehension.

Magic.

Minutes passed.

Magic.

She considered the desiccated corpse sharing her tunnel. His once-studded leather armor was rotted. She found a similarly rotted scabbard for the knife, apparently copper or bronze from the stains on the stone. Been there a long time.

Belt. She found a pouch opposite his scabbard, similarly rotted. It rattled. Metal. Coins? She carefully set the blade down nearby and tugged gently. His belt loops snapped and it fell into her hands. A little metal wire had held a leather tongue in place once. It had rusted and the leather dried.

Jesilyria got both hands around it and pulled gently, like separating an eggshell over a pan. The top popped off in her hand. She set it down and looked in. Her breath caught, froze, refused to exhale from her chest.

Coins.

Not just silver coins, badly corroded by dry time, but four gold coins, stamped with some unknown king's profile.

Äiti might earn the equivalent of an entire gold coin in a year of making little charms and elixirs for neighbors, plus the wool from the sheep fattened up on the high pasture and the odd jobs she had done since the plague had killed Isä and nearly a quarter of the village.

Plague.

Had it really been a punishment from the Herttua for a girl that displeased him? Even here on the mountain she had heard the whispers, discounted them. A Duke couldn't just call down a plague, could he? What if he was a warlock? There had been dark rumors there, too. Scary evil rumors.

Maybe they weren't just rumors.

Maybe she needed to just flee before she became his victim. She was suddenly wealthy beyond girlish dreams. She could fly away.

But who would tend the sheep? She couldn't just leave them up here. And her brother, Jaska, was only six. He couldn't do it. And wouldn't be old enough before she turned sixteen, if she stayed.

The handful of coins called to her like a siren. Jesilyria listened to their song, heard the rocks. She must be practical.

Äiti would know what to do. After all, that's what mothers were for. Especially enchantresses. Äiti The Enchantress.

Jesilyria sighed. Then she pulled the largest gold coin and slid it into her own belt pouch. Practical. And maybe it would spawn others. Maybe they could all three run away to the west, and see the ocean.

Jesilyria stood up with the lantern in one hand, and realized that the man had been leaning against a leather backpack like her own, only much larger and much nicer. Practical called to her. As did the lonely gold coin in her belt pouch. Jesilyria squatted back down and carefully slid the pack away from the wall.

It crumbled as she pulled on the top, so she carefully peeled it back, like an onion. The contents were remarkably similar to her own. Gear for a life lived rough. A blanket. Some rope. A spare tunic. All rotted by time. Strange, unidentifiable metal and leather bits that looked like they had been something important once. A mess kit, with a single tin mug, bowl, and spoon. That was something else the two of them had in common. Every meal eaten alone.

At the bottom, wrapped up in another spare shirt and rotten wool socks, she found two small wooden boxes, rough, but very well made and enameled to survive the passage of time. Neither was heavy. Both were around six inches long, but one was square and the other a slim rectangle maybe four inches on the sides.

Jesilyria opened the larger box first. Inside, she found a large green orb, roughly the size of a goose egg but perfecting spherical, like a soap bubble. She carefully picked it up out of a velvet cradle and held the glass sphere in her hand. Inside it, she could see flickers of movement, like tongues of green flame dancing. On a whim, she picked up the knife and touched the blue orb in the pommel to the green egg. Both glowed, but she knew that would happen. She smiled as she put the orb away. Later.

Jesilyria turned her attention to the smaller box and opened it to find a small black onyx statue, carved in the likeness of a beautiful woman. She held it in one hand and examined it. There was a strange word incised into the base.

When Jesilyria spoke the word, the statue squirmed out of her hand like a wet mouse.

As the statue fell, it transformed into a stunning woman, tall and slender, carved from onyx stone. She danced as she landed, twirling with skill and abandon. She filled the space, leaping gracefully over Jesilyria and the man.

Jesilyria laughed with delight as the woman moved. She spoke the word again and the statue turned, smiled at her, and leapt into the air. It transformed back into the little statue as it flew towards her.

Jesilyria caught it unconsciously in her hand. She smiled, kissed the figurine as a thank you, and carefully put her back in the box. Both boxes were put into Jesilyria's backpack for safe keeping.

Jesilyria carefully rifled through the rest of the man's gear, but everything else was useless. She realized that the body weighed almost nothing, so she carefully wrapped him up in his blanket and carried him to the trunk of the downed tree.

As she shifted everything up onto the tree trunk to leave, Ylwa's head appeared in the opening with a quizzical sound. Trust the dog to be even more practical, keeping watch on the human as well as the sheep.

She climbed up the trunk, with the staffbolt, wrapped body, and lantern precariously balanced in her hands. Beyond the wood, on the other side, she realized that the tunnel turned into stairs down into the darkness.

Giant-made stairs. Long-since forgotten. Perhaps still laden with treasure.

Jesilyria considered her options as she worked her way back into sunlight.

She could turn one of the silver coins into a double handful of copper kopecks and use one to pay one of the younger boys to watch the sheep for a week.

Äiti might forbid her from exploring, especially alone, so she would have to keep everything secret.

Except from Nissa. Nissa would need to know. She would know what to do, as well, about hiring the right boy to watch the sheep and keep his mouth shut. She wasn't as practical as Jesilyria knew herself to be, but she knew people.

Jesilyria reached the top of the downed tree and set her various loads down. She blew out the lantern and carefully drained the reservoir back into the travel flask.

She stared at the black opening leading down to the Giant hall with a new kind of feeling bubbling around in her stomach.

It wasn't smart, or practical, or careful.

It was an adventure.

I originally intended to write a bridge between this book (Volume 2, Fantastic Worlds) and a Volume 3 that was a science fiction collection. My goal was the exact same story, first from the standpoint of one of the locals, and then from the point of the alien who is just a guy doing a job. It turned into something greater along the way, and is one of the stories I'm most proud of, for reasons I won't explain unless you buy me something to drink. Future stories about Doyle are planned, in his further adventures, but I hope you will enjoy a story about the littlest hero.

Greater Than The Gods Intended
Prologue: The Sky

Marasem soared on the morning thermals, stretching his cobalt-blue wings to their utmost. He turned his head a little and snapped his great, spiked tail at an imaginary foe, practicing for the mating flight he knew was due within months.

So many competitors to breed the Empress.

He would need to be strong, as well as crafty. Only the best dragons succeeded. It was finally his time to show the Great Mother his size and power, to become first among equals.

Below, the rugged landscape unfolded slowly like a piece of cloth pushed together, a land only dragons could master. Wyverns, still retaining the original humanoid form of lizardkind, but with wings added, served well to administer for their masters, but could not soar above these mountains. Even the cursed Malakh, simple elves granted feathered wings by the false god, *Mustafa*, were only pale competition.

Only the dragons were meant to rule.

He banked to his right, a wide circle meant to take in the core of his demesne, lest any invaders think to sneak up on him. Dragons could rule, but they needed armies to conquer. Marasem was alone as far as the tremendous eye could see.

Well enough. The mouth of Marasem's aerie gaped before him.

Below, he could see his soldiers. A team of well-trained troglodyte warriors protected the opening, tracking Marasem across the sky with the ancient siege weapon as he closed. He bellowed a challenge at them, watched the weapon turn and lift to cover the sky again behind him. *Paranoia was only prudence in a truly immortal being.*

Marasem banked into a lazy downward spiral and flattened out a few hundred feet above the sharp rocks. He dropped his tail and back-winged to a near stop, and then settled on the ledge gracefully. He took a moment to inspect his troops, and the afternoon sky, before he sauntered into the first entrance and turned sharply around the tight double-corner hidden just inside.

Someday, one of his enemies would think to rush the entrance and swoop into his cave system before the defenders could respond. He smiled at the sound a dragon would make, flying face-first into solid stone at full speed. He even had a recipe prepared for the feast he would throw, keeping the heart for himself while his warriors gorged on his foe.

Chapter 1: The Icon

Youngest Brother held the icon with the utmost reverence. He couldn't resist it when his inner eyelid flickered, once, with pure excitement. Closed. Open. The world went slightly fuzzy for a moment through the membrane. His heart fluttered.

He considered the thing he held. None in the village could understand the words it showed nor the sounds it made, cast so long ago in the ancient tongue. The casing tasted of no material recognized, even among the Yoon clan, respected among all lizardkind, throughout the valley, for the delicacy of their tasting senses.

Eldest Brother stood before him and watched as the spasm of religious excitement and doubts rippled down his body, flaring his scales as though a tremendous heat had passed, and twitching the little stub of tail suddenly against the back of his thigh.

Was he truly worthy to undertake this quest?

But doubt was good. Hadn't the Great Mother taught them that there was always room for doubt, lest one err into arrogance?

And yet...

He could not doubt the surety of this task. For too long, the great lizards, from the Empress Dragon down, had ruled his kind with an iron claw. The troglodytes, at six feet tall, more than twice his own size, practically owned the valley and all the workers and farmers in it. Worse still the Wyverns, for how to make a troglodyte overlord more menacing and arrogant than to give her wings, that she might emulate the Great Mother?

Youngest Brother took a deep breath to settle his nerves. His malachite-colored scales slowly flattened back down. Even the sky grew brighter as his eyes unslitted.

Eldest Brother stared down at him with concern, but also with pride. Two extra inches meant he was the tallest Isaurian in the village, a leader, reinforced by his great cunning. Eldest Brother was very well respected.

He leaned close now to bump snouts with Youngest Brother. "The elders have chosen wisely, Youngest Brother. But always remember that you cannot trust the tall races, nor the scale-less ones. Use them. Abandon them if necessary. Never let them know your true name, lest the evil ones track you here and hurt your family, your village."

Youngest Brother wrapped the icon into a soft leather chamois, and then a rough scrap of cloth. He tucked it into his satchel with care, hidden, and perhaps ignored by a stranger. He smiled a harsh smile, feral. "I would ask the Great Mother to watch over you, Eldest Brother. But that would be wrong, since I seek the tools of vengeance. May you find warm stones and fresh fruit."

Eldest Brother clapped him once on the shoulder as he turned. "Find your luck, Youngest Brother. Find your destiny."

Youngest Brother settled his satchel, his belt, and the straps of his sandals. His shorts were new and well-made leather. They would survive a great journey. He pulled his cape close as he checked the sky. He nodded to himself, and then to Eldest Brother.

He turned and looked at the simple trodden path leading north out of the village. *Thus, the first steps of legend.*

A cry of alarm from the eastern edge of the village ripped the morning sky, followed by bellows of anger and screams of pain.

Both brothers turned towards the sound, and then each other. Youngest Brother was torn by indecision.

Eldest Brother grabbed him by the shoulders and turned him. "The overseers have found us out. You must flee, brother. You must find the tools to free us. Go."

Youngest Brother hesitated yet. The cries came closer. "What of the village?"

Eldest Brother added a soft shove. "If they find the icon, all hope is lost. All the deaths will have been vain."

Youngest Brother took a quick, deep breath. "Then I will become vengeance, Eldest Brother."

He turned and fled into the brush. Behind him, the cries grew terrible.

⁓

Youngest Brother peeked carefully from underneath a large boulder that was perched on a hill overlooking the great rift valley. In the southern distance, he could just make out a ragged column of Isaurian survivors being quick-marched out of the burning remains of the village by a swarm of troglodyte warriors.

Overhead, tiny at this distance, three wyverns in command glided back and forth. Occasional bursts of magic set more fires. Not just the huts, but now the fields were set alight. Youngest Brother cursed silently.

He watched, still as another rock, until all that remained of his kin disappeared from view, eastward around the curve of a hill. Overhead, only birds moved, predators drawn by the smoke and carnage to feast on the remains of Meng'la. In the west, the sun eased behind the mountains.

Youngest Brother took a deep breath to settle his nerves, stretched close to the breaking point after hours of running and hiding.

He reached into his leather satchel and withdrew the crude map of the southern lands, touching the wrapped icon once for luck. His life had new meaning now, even from this morning. This grand quest, this heroic task, had just been escalated from a liberation to a xenocide.

Chapter 2: The Free City

Youngest Brother eyed the public house from an alley across the brick-paved street with suspicion as night slowly enveloped the city. Travelers and locals mingled inside and on the stoop out front. Humans, elves, orcs, and even a semi-mythical creature that was an elf from the waist up attached to the body of a monstrous furred quadruped. Truly, the Free City of Varna was a strange and magical place.

Nineteen days of hard travel and hiding had planed Youngest Brother down, physically as well as emotionally. Half a moon of running from rock to rock during the day and napping at night. Time to digest the deaths. Time enough to learn to live with the grief and anger, but not show it.

Youngest Brother had discovered something about himself, perhaps something Eldest Brother and the village leaders had seen. Commitment to the welfare of others and a willingness to work hard were overlaid now with something else. The memory of smoke. Something he would carry always.

He could still remember the smell, the screams. Youngest Brother had never been consumed by rage. Before now. He clenched his jaw hard and emerged from the alley with a confident, angry stride, crossing the wide boulevard towards the oasis of light and sound. He reached back and touched a long iron knife tucked into the back of his belt to make sure of where it was. He might need it tonight.

Nothing in his life could have prepared Youngest Brother for the inside of the tavern. It was too loud. There were magical lights hanging in every corner and over the bar and above the main room, bringing noon inside night without the acrid, choking smoke of burning black shale.

On a raised dais, a mostly naked orc female, twice his height and easily three times his mass, performed some exotic mating dance that involved the feathers of some gigantic bird and occasionally stomping the hands of patrons that got too close or in her way. Unless coins were tossed onto the platform first. That seemed to make it tolerable for her. Youngest Brother shrugged internally. The unscaled were weird.

He sat perched on a short stool along a back wall and clutched a dirty mug of weak fermented juice. Three pucks, half-sized human-like travelers, strangers to himself as well as each other, joined him at a low shelf designed for creatures three feet tall. Obviously, the bar had a wide clientele. He even suspected that, were he to stay long enough, others of his kind would visit. How would he interact with the out-clan?

Such a strange thought. Out-clan. He was out-clan now. Perhaps clanless. Certainly outlaw, if the troglodytes or their wyvern masters found him.

But humans ruled in the Free City. Longer-lived than troglodytes. Faster-breeding than the elves. Rumored, even, to be the First Race, from whom all others were created by the eldest god, **Mustafa**, The Architect of Heaven; and the Great Mother, **Ailaendae**.

Youngest Brother eyed the largely-human crowd and tried to listen for the voice of destiny. In his pouch, the fate of his kind waited to be unlocked. But he needed a specialist to help decipher the meanings. A scholar conversant in the old tongues. A wizard.

Around him, a seething tide of thieves, whores, fences, assassins, and merchants ebbed and flowed. He sipped his fermented juice.

There. Along the near side wall. A group of humans and troglodytes engaged in a superiority contest. Perhaps another mating ritual to establish breeding dominance. The displays were there. One female, unattached. Six males, three men and two lizardmen loosely arrayed around the sixth, a human male, and the female. Angry words. Threatening postures. Dominance games. They were apparently the same across species.

One of the men reared back and threw a fist at the sixth. The target was taller than the others. Darker-skinned. Exotically dressed. He watched the fist clench and begin to flow.

Youngest Brother heard the stars align.

The sixth growled some strange word, audible over the morass of noise, and raised his left hand. A shield of golden energy appeared magically at his wrist and blocked the incoming punch with a grinding crunch. The first screamed in pain and dropped to his knees.

The entire bar went silent.

Youngest Brother dropped his mug in surprise.

He heard the sixth utter a word and point at one of the troglodytes. A mystic bolt emerged from the man's right hand and struck the surprised target dead-center, blasting him backwards several feet. Number three skidded under a table, unconscious or dead.

The wizard turned to number four and blasted him with the same spell while his eldritch shield protected him from the left side.

Youngest Brother watched the sorcerer square angrily on the last three. His shoulders hunched forward. Fingers twitched as he prepared another deadly spell.

The instigator kneeled on the floor and cradled a broken hand close to his chest. Youngest Brother watched the wizard blast him without pity and then point at the last human and last lizardman standing. He growled. Both raised their hands in submissive posture and backed carefully away.

Youngest Brother forgot his lost drink and remembered to breathe. His inner eyelid nictated once in excitement. Blurry. Clear. Inside, he smiled.

Across the room, the wizard returned to his booth with unchallenged dominance of his mating claim. Youngest Brother watched the woman and tried to evaluate her as breeding stock. Human, so twice his size. Curved of hip and chest in a way that troglodytes or his own kind only rarely achieved. And hair. A strangely-braided reddish rope that seemed to extend to her waist. Perhaps it served as a signal of fertility in the same way an Isaurian's mating crest did. *Interesting.*

Youngest Brother took a deep breath to settle his nerves again and relax his slitted pupils. He touched his satchel once.

Embraced destiny.

Youngest Brother approached the booth politely. Diffidence was too soft. Arrogance was likely to get him struck down by lightning bolts, like the others. Confidence without challenge, then. After all, he was uninterested in mating rights with the female. This was purely a business proposition.

The female watched him draw near with a single raised eyebrow. *How did humans do that?* She leaned closer to the wizard she was snuggled up against and whispered something in his ear. Up close, the wizard had a helmet of curly dark brown hair, cut short, and brown skin the color of fresh khave. He was dressed in pants and a short tunic of some strange material, with a jacket over it that was almost shiny.

The male also raised an eyebrow as he turned to look. *I must learn how they do that. It appears to be a human trick, perhaps a new language.*

Youngest Brother smiled, a gesture he hoped was universal across all sentient races. He didn't get blasted by lightning, so it must be close enough to the human analog.

They stared at each other for a few heartbeats.

Youngest Brother decided to break the silence. "Do you read the ancient tongues?"

Both sets of human eyebrows went up. Youngest Brother flickered his inner eyelid, just to show that he had non-verbal communication methodologies as well. The wizard started, just the slightest bit.

The human scanned the crowd, over and behind Youngest Brother, obviously looking for signs of ambush. A bubble of near silence had emerged around them. Other patrons had not stopped to listen, but had shifted away and quieted, like herd animals just before a storm. A spook might trigger flight. The wizard was rightly feared this night.

The wizard noticed it as well. He leaned in to whisper something in the female's ear and palmed her a coin. She looked disappointed, but slid out of the booth.

The bar crowd parted as she made her way to bar. Youngest Brother shifted so he could keep one eye on the wizard and watch the female move with the other. The crowd seemed poised.

She nodded from the bar and picked up a pitcher of beer.

The wizard slid from the booth, eyed Youngest Brother, and pointed towards the female. "Follow me, please."

Youngest Brother skittered in the human's wake, aware that all noise had now ceased. Truly, the herd thought another storm imminent. He considered windows and other access points he might flee, given the risk.

The female, and then the wizard, passed the end of the giant wooden bar and entered a storage room with a rough table and a number of casks. Youngest Brother followed. The space smelled of dust and fermented grain.

He watched the wizard settle in a chair with his back to the door. The female deposited the pitcher on the table along with two glasses and stepped back. She pulled the door closed, leaving Youngest Brother alone with the wizard.

He was unsure if this was a wise way to end his quest. Or to begin it.

He stood perfectly still as the human studied him. It was an opportunity for him as well, broken though his scholar training had become.

The man finally reached out and poured fermented liquid into one of the mugs. He took a sip. "Which language did you have in mind?"

Youngest Brother paused, lost. *More than one?* He knew of draconic and the common tongue used in the villages and towns for trade. The one he spoke now with the human.

He felt the tip of his tongue slide the least amount out. He remembered humans and troglodytes blasted across the space of the bar by the wizard's eldritch bolts. He played a hunch. "I seek to translate some ancient scripts, but I do not know which language they represent."

The human leaned back in his chair, eyes glittering. Both hands were in view, but that meant nothing. He was a wizard. The silence hung. "Do you have a sample?"

Youngest Brother considered his mistake. If he took out the icon here, the wizard might kill him to steal it. But he had had nothing to scribe the words with, nor reason to do so.

He drew inspiration from the fermented grain beverage. He pointed. "May I?"

The wizards brows moved together. *Truly, Youngest Brother needed to learn that language. Perhaps the female would teach him.*

The wizard slid his chair back from the table a bit and gestured to the other chair.

Youngest Brother climbed onto the chair and reached across to the pitcher. He dipped a finger in the liquid and quickly drew one of the words he remembered onto the wooden surface.

The wizard leaned forward, focused intently. His own tongue tip appeared for the briefest hint.

The human reached inside his jacket and withdrew a small flat rectangle, perhaps two of Youngest Brothers' hands together in length, and more than one in width. He placed it on the table. A small wooden cylinder emerged to join it.

Youngest Brother smelled leather and leaves. So. A book. He had heard stories of such a thing, but his village was too poor to have such treasures. Teaching was oral down the generations, with writing reserved for a few scholars, such as himself.

The wizard flipped the book open. The pages were blank. Youngest Brother was disappointed. The wooden dowel was laid across the paper. "Here."

Youngest Brother considered the dowel. It appeared to be hollow and contain a darker substance. He sniffed it carefully. Hmm. Coal graphite. It would leave a permanent mark on the vegetable substance. *What an useful invention!*

Youngest Brother took the writing device in one hand like a fork and pulled the book closer. Quickly, he scribed as many words and phrases as he could remember from the surface of the icon.

When he finished, he slid the book back to the wizard and rested on his haunches, suddenly tired from the psychic ordeal of his day.

He watched the wizard lift the book and flip randomly through the several marked pages.

The wizard made a strange whistling sound. Youngest Brother nearly fled.

The human stared at him intently. "You are a scribe, no?"

Youngest Brother chewed carefully on the word in his mind. It did not exist in Isaurian, though the roots were there. "I, sir, am a scholar."

The human grinned. At least it looked like a grin. The eyebrows did not move, so perhaps it wasn't. More things to ask the female.

The human laid the book on the table and pointed to one of the strings of symbols. "What you have, my little friend, is a map. This phrase means 'Kunlin Mountain Range' in the most-ancient dialect. It is a place south and west from here."

Youngest Brother put on a serious face, but inwardly, he giggled with delight. The legends were true. "I see. And what would you charge to translate the rest of the terms?"

He watched the human lean back in his chair and take a slow drink from the mug. The level of the fluid did not appear to alter appreciably. It felt like a game of dragon-chess with Eldest Brother. He comported himself accordingly.

Time passed.

The wizard leaned forward. "How about a different option?"

Youngest Brother attempted to cock his head at an angle, similar to the way he had seen the two humans interact. Apparently, it worked.

The human smiled and pointed at another word-string. "I am extremely interested in learning more about this map. This is the ancient word *depot*. It means a place where the ancients often stored weapons. Perhaps a few survive."

Youngest Brother's inner eyelid flickered. Shut. Open. He cursed such a loss of control before his negotiating foe.

The wizard apparently took it as a hopeful sign. "I propose a partnership. You and I. Your map. My...wizardry. Perhaps we recruit a few experts. Then we go see if there are any weapons there. Your thoughts?

Youngest Brother was almost too stunned to think. He sputtered. "But you are a wizard. Wizards do no put themselves at risk. They live in tall towers and research great thoughts."

The human smiled at him. "And they don't get into bar fights."

Youngest Brother made a moue. *True.* This one did not fit the pattern of wizards from the old tales. "Why would you do this thing?"

The human grew serious. One finger tapped the tabletop. "Many reasons. Wealth. Power. Knowledge. And I really don't like dragons."

Youngest Brother felt his toes tingle and try to curl under. Could this wizard be an ally against the great ones? It was true that the war between the great ones and the scaleless was ancient. The Sky Empire and the Empire Of The West had fought many wars. Only along the fringes were the lesser races able to carve out a kind of space between the elves and the troglodytes, and their overlords. And their gods.

He tried a different tack. "How would we pay for these *experts*? I have very little cash to hire people."

The man smiled. "Ah, but you have the map. It has the potential for great value. Among my kind, there is a term called *sweat equity*. I will contribute gold to the partnership. You will bring information. We will share the rewards equally."

Youngest Brother had never heard it called such a thing, but the poor villagers of his clan understood *barter*. From each according to his ability. To each according to his needs. "How do you know such things?"

The man took a real drink of his beverage this time. "Before I was a wizard, in a land far, far away, I was a merchant."

Youngest Brother shuddered at such a terrible disgrace. "What of your mate?"

The human cocked his head and raised an eyebrow. Again, the language of face muscles.

Youngest Brother suppressed the need to practice the movements. "The female. Your consort. The one guarding our privacy."

"Ah. Irsh. Actually, I was considering hiring her to join us. She is a thief, not a prostitute, although she occasionally is mistaken for the latter."

Youngest Brother could not resist mirroring the cocked head. *Practice, of course.* "Why would a wizard need a thief? Is your magic insufficient?"

Youngest Brother braced for a lightning bolt, surprised by the sudden audacity of his tongue.

The human laughed. "Rarely. But she is a wonderful source of gossip. And occasionally, bad men need to have bad things happen to them."

"Only bad men?"

The human's smile grew immense. "Ethics, my little friend, are what you do when no one is looking."

The scaleless were weird. "I see. I believe such a partnership is acceptable. How shall we proceed?"

He watched the wizard move the pitcher and the mugs to the side and dry the tabletop with a sleeve. "Can I see the device?"

Youngest Brother felt his insides freeze solid. *How? But...* He prevaricated. "What device?"

The human pointed a finger at his satchel. "The one in your bag. I detected it with my...magic...when we entered the room."

Yes. Of course. A wizard. And yet... "But you did not take it. Even though you could have?"

The wizard grew very serious. "This planet will never advance, as long as the mighty terrorize the meek. An Isaurian rebel seeking dragon-slaying weapons is a cause I find noble. Which reminds me. What is your name, my friend?"

Youngest Brother remembered Eldest Brother's words about trusting the scaleless. "You could not pronounce it. Call me *Partner*."

"Very well, Partner. My full name is Doyle Iwakuma. You should call me Doyle."

Youngest Brother touched his first human as they shook hands across the scarred wood. Scaleless flash felt like fresh leather. It was strangely warm and vaguely moist. "That is a very strange name. Where are you from?"

The wizard, Doyle, smiled in a detached, knowing manner. "Farther away than could probably imagine, my friend."

Youngest Brother, *Partner*, nodded. "I see." He would, eventually, but could not have dreamed it that day.

Chapter 3: Travails

"Remind me again, Partner, why we have to walk there?"

The warrior, Sachesu, enjoyed calling him by that name, even though his partnership was with the wizard Doyle and the warrior was an *employee,* to quote the wizard's odd term.

At nearly eight feet tall, the ogre was nearly three times Youngest Brother's height, and at least five times his mass. According to Doyle, the ogres were created by the first god, *Mustafa*, to provide overseers for the orcs, much as angels for the elves and pucks and dwarves, or troglodytes for his own kind. But this ogre treated Youngest Brother with respect and humor.

The human woman, Irshandra ("Call me Irsh.") did as well. It must be a custom among the scaleless. Wyverns and troglodytes would be jockeying with their own kind for edge and social stature constantly. Perhaps it was safe here because they represented three different species, plus a wizard?

Youngest Brother decided to attempt humor. It was a novel method of communication for him. Troglodytes were very literal. "Because the terrain is too rough for mounts, and ogres apparently cannot fly. This must have been an oversight obviously corrected when the gods made the angels and the wyverns, Sachesu."

The ogre turned to him with a look of stunned disbelief, met a grin, grinned back. The grin became laughter. "No, Partner, I am not a magus. Otherwise, I would be a king."

The female who-was-not-Doyle's-mate chimed in. "Just as well. You'd be a horrible king. I like him, Doyle. Very few people can make an ogre laugh."

Doyle crested a rise and looked out at the rough, semi-arid canyon climbing away from the group. "Sach, this looks like a good enough place to camp. Let's find some shelter. We've got about another day, day and a half, in front of us."

Youngest Brother, *Partner* now, watched the wizard pull out a scroll tube of maps from his pack as he settled on a nearby rock outcrop. Uncorked, one would find the seven pieces of parchment and vellum, laboriously copied from the icon's faces and projections, what Doyle had called a *nav beacon* in the ancient tongue.

Carefully, Doyle selected one sheet, slid the rest home, and unrolled it on the rock.

Partner grabbed the far edge to keep it flat and sat down to study the map, upside down from him. Not that he needed to. All the time he had spent transcribing images and runes from the icon had required that he memorize every facet on the map in its relation.

The canyon they traversed was an arroyo that existed on both the ancient map and on more current versions. According to the wizard, that meant it had not changed much in more than four thousand years, nor had the ancient volcanic tor that had been hollowed by the magic of the ancients. The insides would not change much for ten thousand more.

Getting there, however, and finding one of the entrances, would be troublesome.

Partner felt Irsh lean over his shoulder to look. "Where are we?"

Doyle studied the map, so Partner put a finger down, a little east of center. "Here."

She examined it for a moment more. "And the cave?"

He shifted his finger farther south and east, tracing the line of the ravine until it began to flatten out on a plateau. "Somewhere here. It may be buried and require excavation."

Sachesu joined now, lurking over everyone, careful to stay out of the afternoon light. "What if the dragons destroyed it?"

Doyle smiled up at him. "It's made of mithral steel, Sach. Among the dragons, breathing ice, fire, or poison gas won't even scratch it. Maybe one of the acid-spitters could do it, if he wanted to spend ten years at the task. And even then, he's more likely to destroy the rocks around it that the metal."

"And the whole thing is made of mithral?" The ogre's eyes lit up with greed. "How much?"

Doyle shrugged. "The ancients had great powers. Probably tons of it."

Irsh whistled. "Just to make a door."

Doyle gave her a serious look. "Probably a door wide enough to drive two wagons and teams of horses through, and a hallway beyond. They built on a grand scale."

Partner sighed. "How far we have fallen. Today, a sliver of such metal to make a tool or weapon costs more than my village would have earned in a year. We must fix this."

Doyle put a friendly hand on his shoulder. "We are, Partner. Small steps."

Sachesu, ever practical, cleared his throat in an announcing way. "Which reminds me. Partner, how well can you fight?"

Partner looked up at the gigantic warrior as if he had suddenly grown a tail. He looked down to check. "I am a scholar, a keeper of the oral histories. I have never fought."

"Thought not." The ogre reached into his pack and pulled out a tiny knife in a sheath. It was perhaps the length of his hand. He handed it to Partner.

Partner took the blade, as long as his cubit, and considered it scientifically. "I cannot use this, Sachesu, though I thank you for the effort. I would not know how to engage."

He tried to hand it back, but the ogre caught his hand and engulfed it in his huge paw. "You will need to learn, Partner. Someday, it may mean your life."

Sachesu delicately arranged Partner's fingers and hand around the grip. Partner expected the giant to grind his bones, but the touch was feather light. "You hold it like that. Blade forward, parallel to the ground. You can stab or slash with it."

"But I am a scholar."

"All the better, Partner. Nobody would expect you to be dangerous. And you don't have to worry about the edge catching on bone. It's mithral steel, magically honed to a razor edge."

Sachesu carefully caught the tip of the sheath and removed it, leaving the silvery dagger bare.

Partner studied the metal, and his reflection in it. The value of the metal was immense. The friendship, even greater. "Thank you, Sachesu. I shall endeavor to be worthy."

Irsh leaned close to study the little dagger. "And I need to teach you to throw it properly."

Partner was aghast. "You can throw a knife?"

Nearby, he watched Doyle swallow a laugh before Irsh could wipe the shocked look from her face. She sputtered instead.

Doyle came to her rescue. "Indeed, Partner. But this is not the best place to learn. When we return to the lowlands where there are many more trees. Perhaps we can find you a cactus tomorrow."

Partner studied the blade again, contemplated a mechanism whereby he could use it as a thrown weapon. It would not fly like a rock, it would tumble. And it was not long enough to remain stable like an arrow or javelin. He felt like he was the butt of another practical joke, only this time from his companions instead of his brother. "I do not see how."

Irsh smiled. "Like this." She pulled a similar weapon from her own belt, flipped it over to hold the tip between fingers and threw it overhand.

Partner watched it tumble in a circle that ended with the blade driven hilt-deep into what appeared to be a desert hare, that had been sitting perfectly still, fifteen feet away.

It quivered for the briefest moment. The blade, not the rabbit.

Partner was ever-so-slightly daunted. "I see."

Perhaps the scaleless were more dangerous than he realized.

Or the quest was, and he was only now realizing it.

⌁

"Sachesu, please stand perfectly still."

Partner caught the ogre's eyes to reinforce the message, and then slowly moved clockwise around the giant warrior.

Sachesu froze in place. Only his eyes moved. And one eartip. "Yes, Partner?"

Partner examined a spot on the rockwall just ahead of Sachesu. He got down on his hands and knees and thrust his snout even lower to get a good view.

Behind him, Doyle called out. "Partner?"

Partner could hear the strain in the voice, echoing softly in the utter silence of the dry ravine. He rocked back onto his heels and rotated just his head to look back over a shoulder. "We appear to have arrived."

The wizard stopped the hand reaching for a map. "Oh?"

"Indeed. Sachesu is standing on a deadfall trap that will drop him into a hunting pit."

He heard the female from farther back. "How can you be sure, Partner?"

He smiled grimly. "Because it is the same kind my village used to use to capture large ungulates."

Partner considered the device again. He made a face as he thought about how to disarm it, then lit up with a smile. "Sachesu, thank you for helping me save your life."

The ogre barely even breathed. "Huh?"

Partner pulled the fine little dagger from his satchel and slid the tip into a tiny crack in the rocks until the tip stopped. "Sachesu, please take a long step backwards and to your left. Wizard Doyle, please grab his arm if he begins to slide into the earth. I believe I have disarmed the device, but there will be only one way to be sure."

Partner watched the giant meekly stride towards the others. As he did, there was an audible click followed by a quiet metallic thump. Partner smiled to the others with delight.

They all remained frozen in place.

Irsh moved to her left to get a better view. "Is it safe?"

Partner stood. He bent and used a finger to trace a perfectly straight line in the sandy dirt. "Perfectly, Lady Irsh. And if we are careful, we should be able to enter the burrow via this machine. How much rope do we possess?"

Doyle approached, working his way around the deadfall instead of crossing it.

Partner watched him pull a wand from his belt. It was a short, squat, stubby wand, perhaps more like a knobby book than a wand, once he thought about it for a moment.

Doyle made careful arcane passes in the continuing silence. "Huh. Completely non-magical."

Partner nodded at his partner. "Indeed, Doyle. It is entirely mechanical in nature. A very common design."

He squatted down and quickly sketched in the dirt, a machine with pulleys, gears, and plates.

Irsh had crept close enough to view. A finger pointed. "What are those?"

Partner glanced up. She was paying close attention. The ogre still had not moved. He lowered his voice a bit. "Those are the spears that would impale the creature falling into the trap."

She nodded. "I see. And how do we get down there safely?"

Partner pointed to the knife wedged into the trigger. "The drop is open. Only the mithral strength of the steel kept it from being sheared off and opening the pit. Once we remove the cotter pin, the way will open and we can climb down. There will be space. As I said, my own village used a similar device to catch large game animals."

A very quiet ogrish voice. "Is it safe, Partner?"

Partner stood and leaned to get a clear view. He pointed to the safe path. "Indeed, friend Sachesu. Please step there and join us."

Irsh turned to the wizard. "Doyle? What do you think?"

Doyle thought for a moment. "Good as any. Knew we were close. Hopefully these caves connect to the place we're looking for. Let's do it."

She nodded and pulled her backpack off. Rope appeared, as did a lantern with a magical, ever-glowing stone. A cloak with a strange, almost shifting pattern of subtle colors, draped across her shoulders.

Irsh added a bandolier with several small knives protruding next. More knives got tucked into boots, belt, and a small one tucked inside of the gap her cleavage produced in her armored shirt. More were added to bracers on both wrists, suggesting ambidexterity in a manner Partner found most unsettling.

These people below were his kind. Obviously, they would welcome visitors, wouldn't they?

He grew further unsettled as Doyle checked several esoteric magic items of likely offensive and defensive capabilities. Sachesu dug a blue buckler the size of Partner's chest from his backpack and strapped it on his wrist, along with a helmet that had a magically glowing gem set in the forehead.

Had he signed up for a small war? "Friend Doyle, is all this warlikeness necessary? Can we not negotiate with the local tribe for their assistance?"

The wizard looked down at him confused for a moment. "Partner, many of the tribes in these hills do not consider it cannibalism to eat humans and ogres."

"Truly?"

Partner was intrigued at such behavior. So unlike his now-lost village. And his scholarly training was intrigued. *What did ogre taste like, anyway?* He shrugged.

Partner checked his satchel and adjusted the scabbard of his little knife on his belt, just to fit in with his more-bellicose associates. "Are we in readiness?"

Each nodded in turn.

Partner gripped the little knife and pulled.

Nothing happened.

He pulled again.

The blade remained stubbornly wedged in place.

Hmph.

"Sachesu, may I impinge upon your greater musculature to withdraw the weapon from the blocking mechanism?"

The ogre stepped close and leaned over. *Garlic and pepper breath.*

A paw engulfed the blade.

Nothing moved.

The ogre looked up and whistled. "This will take some work. It is in there tight."

Sachesu paused, seated himself, and braced a foot against the stone wall. Both hands gripped and pulled with a growl.

The blade popped clear.

The trapdoor hinged open with a silent suddenness.

Sachesu began to tumble over backwards into the fifteen foot drop. Partner flopped awkwardly across the ogre's shin guards, pinned the ankles down until he could put a hand down and stop his fall.

"Whoa."

Partner was unsure who spoke. Both Doyle and Irsh looked into the revealed pit.

Rows of two-foot-long spears set into the floor rusted in the dry air, like rotting teeth.

Sachesu lifted Partner to his feet and stood. "Thank you, Partner. What do we think?"

Doyle turned to them with an ominous stare. "Looks like the mouth of hell."

Chapter 4: Underground

Partner considered the tunnel's dimensions, decided it must have been cut for humans. *Cut?* Yes, the walls were perfectly straight and cleanly smooth, with an arching peak. Sachesu was able to walk down the center without ducking. His own kind would have made warrens with four foot ceilings. Troglodytes would have preferred narrower walls. Wyverns would have made them wider.

And the magic down here was palpable.

Strips set flush into the roof glowed with a sharp, white light as they approached, and then faded after they passed. It was so unlike sunlight as to make his scales turn almost mint-colored. The air had a clean, post-rain feel that suggested magically-powered fans pushing it around, rather than the stale musk of his home caverns

But no people.

No dust covered the floor to raise footprints. No spiders wove webs in corners, but there were no insects either.

"Wizard Doyle, I have a question that requires your experience with magic to grasp."

Up front, at the head of the their little column, Doyle paused and stepped back around Sachesu's massive bulk. Behind, Partner glanced and saw Irsh take a few steps away to drift into the dusky darkness.

"Yes, Partner? What's on your mind?"

Partner pointed at the upper edge of a nearby wall. "Since we have descended into the earth, I have seen no other creatures besides ourselves, including the basest insects. I would have expected... something."

He watched the wizard pull another magical device, the shape and size of a large, flat river stone, from his belt and hold it in the air, making passes like a priest sprinkling holy water on the faithful. The ritual magic was utterly fascinating. It felt like home.

Partner suppressed a pang of longing.

Doyle finished his ritual and returned the item to a belt pouch. "Interesting. Partner, you're correct. I can detect no other *lifeforms* beyond ours."

Lifeforms? "Lifeforms, wizard Doyle?"

The human smiled wryly. "One ogre, two humans, one isaurian. Nothing else as far as I can scan."

Scan? The scaleless were weird enough, wizards just made it worse.

Irsh appeared at a silent jog, lights flickering on and off as she moved. She paused as she came even. "Someone coming. Behind us."

Partner turned with the rest. He could hear a strange hissing rumble in the sudden quiet, but no ceiling lights marked the creature's progress.

He watched fascinated as Doyle pulled a vial from his belt and twisted it without breaking the material. Something popped. Two good shakes to mix the contents and it began to softly glow. "How it that done, Doyle?"

The human glanced down, grinned, and snapped the vial down the hallway with a hard underhanded toss. "Alchemy."

"Ah. Of course."

Downrange, the glowing vial tumbled to a halt. It waited forlornly in a small puddle of yellow-green light. It was not lonely for long.

A creature emerged from the darkness. Partner thought of a giant land tortoise, but this creature traveled on what appeared to be black wheels instead. It rolled to a stop a few feet short of the glowing vial and appeared to consider it for several seconds.

Doyle reacted first. "Oh, crap. Everyone run. This way."

The human took off at a jog away from the creature. Partner followed, aware of how dangerous tortoises were on the surface to his kind. Behind, he heard Sachesu begin to trot. Irsh never made a sound when she moved.

The ogre called softly as he caught up, long loping strides more than making up for Doyle's headstart. "Doyle, what was that thing?"

Doyle glanced back, but kept his attention forward. He seemed hard pressed to find the right word as Partner watched. "Call it a golem. Close enough."

Partner was even more fascinated. "A golem? Really? How exciting!"

Doyle kept moving. "Sure, if you think an immortal, nearly-unkillable machine designed to keep things out of these tunnels is fun. We need to outrun it."

Partner was deeply pained. "I am a scholar, not an athlete. This is the greatest speed I can attain. If need be, you should sacrifice me to protect the others."

Sachesu swooped up close. "Your pardon, Partner. Can't do that."

The ogre grabbed him around the waist and lifted him into the air, much as an adult would carry an infant. It was extremely efficient, if a bit demeaning.

Immediately, the group began moving at a greater clip.

Partner took advantage of his vantage point to study the tunnel. "Doyle, we are approaching another of those strange sliding doors that you referred to as an *blast barrier* before. If the creature is intent on pursuing us, perhaps we could seal that door and use your magic to disable the mechanism, thereby trapping it here?"

They continued to run.

Doyle pulled up as he crossed the line carved in the metal floor. "Irsh, see if you can find a lock we can seal. I don't want to trap ourselves in on the wrong side if we don't have to."

Sachesu paused and set Partner carefully down. "Is that thing really unkillable, Doyle?"

The wizard explored one wall as Irsh took the other side of the hall. "That model is extremely rugged. It was built to keep the tunnels clear of debris and do basic maintenance."

Partner considered the term. *Model?* That suggested many of them rather than a single demon made metallic flesh, such as the wyverns always threatened to conjure. *Interesting.*

Irsh punched a button triumphantly. "Got it."

The door rattled closed with a hiss and a bang. Irsh continued to address strangely colored magical runes that glowed in the wall at human height.

Partner could not make sense of the colors nor the strange writing, but something was happening. He felt his ears suddenly pop. "What is that feeling?"

Irsh shrugged. "I learned that trick on a set of ruins in the human lands. It keeps the door from being opened by someone on the other side."

Partner considered it. "I see. But why do my ears feel stiff?"

Doyle inspected the panel closely. "Overpressure. Sealed against gas attacks so the atmosphere is charged as a defense mechanism."

Partner recognized the words. Each of them. They even strung together nicely. They still made no sense. He paused to consider them some more.

Doyle seemed satisfied with the runes. "It will hold for now. We need to move quickly. I'm not sure how smart the...golem is."

Sachesu approached politely. "Partner, my apologies for before. Would it acceptable to convey you at speed again?"

Partner blinked both sets of eyelids in surprise. *Ogres didn't have manners. All the tales agreed on that point. But still.* "Of course, Sachesu. Thank you."

It was only proper. Death might still be on their heels.

It was another door. Another closed *blast barrier* blocked their path. Two others had surrendered to Irsh's patient and nimble fingers and been sealed up again behind them. Doyle seemed excited that the magic controlling them was still intact after so long.

Partner was not sure he shared the human's enthusiasm. Dragons were also immortal.

He joined a kneeling Doyle to study one of the hand-drawn maps. The wizard had augmented this one extensively from what he called the *standard design architecture* of the ancients. It showed a warren of perfectly straight lines intersecting perfect arcs of a circle, like a student's lesson in geometry. So unlike his own kind.

Partner considered the tunnels they had traversed to this point. One cave-in had blocked them, but a side tunnel had been available after a short backtrack. More recently, the tunnels were more poorly lit and dusty, so perhaps the golem was unable to pursue them thus. By now, they should be reaching close to the center of the mountain.

The sound of Irsh's palm slapping the metallic panel in disgust got everyone's attention. Partner was unsure of the word that accompanied it, although he suspected it was one impolite for proper company. He did not press her to repeat it.

Doyle stood and stretched. "Locked?"

She shrugged eloquently. "The magic has been dispelled. There is damage to the wall, so maybe an earth-shift has broken something. I can't get it to do anything."

Doyle smiled and approached. Partner ghosted along in his wake.

Partner watched the wizard draw out his little divination tool from his belt again and cast some spell on the door. Nothing happened, regardless of the gestures employed, so Partner was inclined to agree with the blade-throwing female.

Doyle joined their conclusion. "Yup. Dead. Good thing you brought along a wizard. Hopefully, we can get the casing open and locate a *manual override* or *crosswire* the *primary power supply*. Let me take a look."

Partner had learned that the wizard frequently fell into a very strange arcane cant when he worked. He sometimes recognized words from the ancient tongue, and was learning a tremendous amount. The troglodyte masters and their wyvern overlords would be doomed if he could find the tools to fight them, especially the fire wands they used to kill and destroy from range.

Doyle pulled a strangely-shaped instrument from another pouch on his belt. It was round, like a crowbar, with a flat tip at one end, but only a human hand long. The other end had a strange, crystalline grip.

Partner was puzzled, until he watched Doyle fit the chisel tip into a small slot in one corner and twist. Something moved. As the wizard twisted more, a round piece of metal rose out of a hole.

When the little metal cylinder fell free, Partner's inner eyelids flickered. *Magic! The darkest arts.*

Doyle moved on to another corner of the lock and found a second slot. Partner realized that each corner had such a slot. Each surrendered to the wizard's patient hands.

Partner held his breath as Doyle removed the last slotted cylinder. The entire face of the lock came free with a twist of the chisel-tip. Doyle handed it down to Partner, standing so patiently quiet next to him. "Partner, could you set this down for me? I need to get to the innards of the lock."

Partner rested this new icon on the floor well away from their feet and studied the strange locking mechanism. It had no gears or pullies. Instead, the interior was a strange green color, with bumps and shapes in other colors, and golden threads binding it all together.

Doyle looked down. "Careful. It's about to get dusty."

Partner flicked his inner eyelids closed as the human took a breath and blew sharply into the device. For good measure, he closed his nostrils as well. It was just as well. There was a great deal of dust. Apparently, the land tortoise was entirely absent.

As the dust passed, Partner studied the device. The golden threads were marred near one corner. He pointed without touching. "Friend Doyle, has the device been damaged by an insect?"

Doyle leaned down to get a better view. He muttered a spell and pointed his right index finger, just as he had at the bar that night. This time, a white light appeared where he pointed.

Partner was thrilled. It was a different spell than the one he had cast before. Partner might yet learn the arcane arts, given enough time.

Doyle stuck his left hand closed and rubbed at the damaged spot. "Good eyes, Partner. Something took a bite of the *plastic* before deciding it didn't like the taste."

Partner smiled at the compliment. "It is reparable?"

He watched the human trace the golden threads both directions with a finger while muttering more arcanums under his breath. Doyle worked his way down to a silver circle in the opposite corner that he tapped. "Hmm."

Partner shifted himself a little to the side to watch unobtrusively as the wizard took off his backpack and pulled out a wrapped leather satchel and unwound it on the floor. Inside were all manner of small metal tools, many looking like alien insects frozen and then cast.

The human picked one that ended in a strange circular claw and measured it against the silver circle. With more muttering, he brought the claws to life and pressed them forward.

Partner watched rapt as the claws seemed to sniff at the thing and slowly embrace it, flowing and molding themselves into small gaps and biting down. Never had he imagined *magic* like this. Perhaps his kind should have more travels to the lands of the scaleless.

After several moments, all of the claws had achieved purchase. They seemed to all pull at the same moment and the silver circle popped free to reveal the cylinder as a disk two fingers across and a fingernail thick.

As Doyle withdrew the magical metal creature, the claws lost their grip and the disk fell, Partner's hand flashed out and snatched it out of the air, much like an errant insect. It was extremely cool to the touch. The back was a smooth black material that was neither metal nor wood, inset with two smaller metal disks that seemed to be made of gold.

He presented it on an open palm. "Doyle?"

The wizard reached down carefully to pick it up. "Thank you, Partner. You seem to be good luck."

Irsh piped up at that moment. "We knew that. Hey, Doyle? Are we likely to be here for a while?"

Partner watched the human weigh the costs of his magic carefully. They were in a dead end, if something like the iron turtle came, but this was also possibly the last door before the innermost nest of the mountain.

Doyle looked up from the thing he held. "Maybe an hour, if I can fix this."

She cocked her head at him. "What's an hour?"

"Sorry. Long enough to fix some food and some tea, or take a nap, but not longer than that."

She walked up behind the ogre and began rifling through his oversized pack. "Tea, coming up. And some flatcakes with jam."

Partner crossed his ankles and sat to watch the wizard at work. So much to learn.

⌒

Doyle snapped the little silver disk from some strange new device with one hand as he sipped tea with the other. He handed it back to the strange silver insect and pressed it against the lock device.

It writhed for a moment, and then settled with a loud click.

Partner's inner eyelid flickered with delight.

He watched the wizard trace the golden threads back to the previously-marred corner that had been repaired with new threads Doyle carried in his tool satchel.

A small green light flickered to life, happy, in the center of the thing.

Doyle smiled. "And it will hold a charge. Not sure how long, but we should be good."

Partner understood every word the human spoke, and not one meaning. It must be awkward to be so far removed from everyday people concerns.

Doyle pressed a finger against a large red circle in one corner while muttering. The words seemed to be profanities instead of arcana, but sometimes it was hard to differentiate.

Nothing happened for a moment, and then a faint grinding sound was audible.

Partner leapt to his feet as the large door, the *blast barrier*, moved. But it only traveled a few inches before it froze in place. Doyle muttered more arcana. Or profanities.

Partner leaned close to the opening and sniffed at the slight breeze coming out. It smelled more like home than these tunnels had. Earthy. Warm. Lizardy. And dragon. Perhaps the adventure had truly just begun.

Behind him, he heard the wizard raise his voice to conversational levels. "Sach, we'll need your crowbar and muscles now."

The ogre laughed. "Nobody ever loves me for my mind."

Irsh laughed as well. "Perhaps you should take up philosophy then."

Sachesu's laugh boomed. "The world is not prepared for an ogre of letters. Remind me when we get home. Your pardon, Partner. Oversized thug must earn his pitiful keep now."

Partner stepped back with a grin to watch as the giant wedged the tip of a monstrous chunk of black metal into the gap. The crowbar easily outweighed him, but Sachesu handled it like a wand. Sachesu leaned into the tool with a grunt.

The door moved another two handspans before it stopped.

Partner watched Doyle reach into his pack and pull out a small metal cylinder colored a rich blue, with a strange red crown. He shook the vial a few times and stepped close to the door near the center. Doyle pressed the crown and unleashed a small spray of a golden-brown fluid that flowed into the door jamb. It smelled of the strange coal brought up from the deepest mines.

Doyle stopped and looked up. "Try it now, Sach."

The ogre took a deep breath and flexed. The door suddenly slid several feet before binding. Even dropping the crowbar and pushing directly in the gap, Sachesu could not move it. "Looks like that's it."

Doyle carefully returned the small sprayer to his belt. "Good enough. What's on the other side?"

Partner had stepped through, even as Sachesu had tried to move the door, the benefit of being small. The far side was dark. The floor was several inches higher, covered in smooth dirt that smelled old and stale. Partner knelt down and dug with one finger to confirm his suspicion. Underneath he found the same silver-white metal hallway that his companions had been traversing.

Partner touched a wall as well. It was the same metal as well, but covered in dirt and oily grime, as through years of oil lamps had left their smoky deposit. Or perhaps centuries. The air had that kind of dead, stale smell to it.

There was also darkness. The ceiling lights that had magically activated and faded as he had moved were absent here. Covered? Damaged? Removed? He would need the ogre's great height and Doyle's magical lamp to be sure. It was good to have useful friends. He heard them arrive behind him.

Irsh was apparently first through the gap. Her lamp was barely enough to augment what came through. "Partner?"

He turned, aware that the light would glow off his inner eyes. Even in his mind, the words sounded ominous. "We must exercise great care, Irsh."

He watched her unconsciously touch one of the many knives on her left wrist. "Why is that, Partner?"

The others joined them as he spoke. "There is a dragon in these tunnels."

The lighter-skinned, red-haired Irsh paled. Doyle's skin took on a grayer pallor as Partner watched. "Are you sure?"

Partner nodded. He had seen the signs in his companions before, but this confirmed it. "It is an unmistakable smell. Perhaps too subtle for your kinds, but obvious to mine. Fortunately, he has not been in this part of the warren in a very long time. Perhaps since he was very young, and much smaller."

Irsh sniffed hard. "I smell...something. Can you tell the color? And are you sure it is male?"

Partner shook his head. "I can only presume. Most dragons are male. The Great Mother, *Ailaendae,* the First Dragon, designed the lizard races to have a very different gender balance from the scaleless."

Sachesu looked confused. "The scaleless?"

A human would have blushed. Partner felt his scales flare out from his skin in embarrassment. "My apologies, Sachesu. It was an impolite term my kind uses to describe those children of the First God, *Mustafa,* that he chose to make in his own image. Unlike lizardkind. Scaleless. As a philosopher, is there a better term to use?"

Sachesu paused. "I do not know, Partner. We tend to call everyone humanity, to reflect our common heritage. Though I do not know how many races can cross-breed, beyond the half-elves who are commonly mules. I will give this thought."

Partner flattened his scales down, redeemed in the knowledge that he was a friend of the first great ogre philosopher, as far as he knew. Truly, the world was changing.

Doyle reached up and pulled a gem on a gold chain from his tunic, revealing the edge of a mail shirt underneath. He touched the back once and the gem began to glow with a soft white glow. "Partner, I think you should lead, since you have the best nose. The chambers we seek should be close."

Partner felt his face grow serious. "Indeed, Doyle."

He moved to the center of the dirty-covered hallway and contemplated the darkness. There was a dragon in these tunnels. A dragon he intended to kill.

Chapter 5: The Dragon's Den

Partner found the smell almost overwhelming. The air seemed to hang with a taste he thought he could chew, earthy and lizardy all at once. Dragonmusk.

He crept along a small side hallway, carved by his own kind, rather than the ancients or the troglodytes. The signs were there. A smooth finish to three feet, and then rougher to a ceiling eight or nine feet overhead, perhaps four or six inches narrower at the top than the bottom. Textured floors cut with shallow grooves on each side of the tunnel to channel any water to the edges and away from walking feet.

Troglodyte tunnels tended to be perfectly square vertically, and lack the drain channel, since they never had to clean after any flood or springleak. They also moved in straight lines, rather than following natural seams in the stone.

After nearly a day in the tunnels of the ancients, this tunnel felt cramped, where he would have once called it homelike. And it smelled strange. Old. Forgotten. Stale. But the dragonmusk was strong.

Partner stopped and took a deep breath. He had never smelled dragonmusk before, but his mind knew the flavor. Perhaps Ailaendae had programmed it into her followers when she made them. Dragonfear. Partner settled his scales and took another two steps to a soft corner.

His nose detected a breeze blowing toward him. The musk was stronger now. Perhaps even enough for Doyle or Sachesu to smell it and understand. He must be close. He peeked around.

He felt his inner eyelids flicker uncontrollably for a second.

Below, an image made him want to fall to his knees in worship.

Partner barely stopped himself from crying out in sudden ecstasy. Below him, looking down from the ledge he found himself on, stretched out on the warm sands, lay a tremendous dragon, resplendent blue scales glowing in lamp light.

A voice whispered in his ear, unbidden.

It persisted, demanded attention, worship. It overawed his mind, except for one little corner that cataloged the entire affair scientifically, and another corner that complained loudly at such effrontery.

The dragon captured him, unknowing.

Another voice intruded. A different voice. Quiet. Pleading. Penetrating. The awake parts of his mind responded impotently. The rest continued to venerate.

Something intruded on his breathing. Insistent. Something wrapped around his nostrils, blocked them shut. Tried to choke him.

Partner turned to look at what was attacking him, found Irsh hovering silently beside him, one hand pinching the end of his snout. *How long had he been frozen?*

She looked a question at him, concern written on her features. The language of face muscles he had been learning from her.

Partner understood, nodded.

She released the grip on his nose, put a finger to her lips to indicate silence, and moved deeper into the caverns, where the rest waited. A thoroughly-chastened Isaurian scholar followed.

Around several curves and safely removed, Doyle and Sachesu rested. Doyle held one of his Witchfinder artifacts in one hand, studied the ebb and flow of the arcana under this mountain. Sachesu sipped cold tea from a flask and appeared to think philosophical thoughts. At least, that was what the ogre had taken to telling everyone.

Doyle looked up. "We were beginning to get worried."

Partner felt all of his scales flare in embarrassment again. "It is worse than I imagined. When the Great Mother made the lizard races, she programmed dragonfear and dragonworship into us. I saw him, wizard Doyle, the wyrm who is the overlord of these tunnels, and wanted nothing more than to worship him. I could watch it in my mind, but not fight it."

Irsh joined him as he sat. She touched his shoulder with a friendly hand. "Can you breathe through your mouth?"

Partner felt his mind upend. "Can I what?"

She persisted. "Your mouth. Could you breathe if your nostrils were blocked?"

Partner nodded, unsure at the line of questioning.

Irsh smiled. "Because when I found you, your nostrils were flared open as far as they could go and you were snorting like a horse. You said the power is in the smell. So we need to ruin your sense of smell for a while."

Partner-the-scholar laughed with delight in his mind. Partner-the-dragon-worshipper wanted to go back. Partner-the-adventurer voted against the addiction. "Very good. How do we do such a thing?"

He watched her pull a length of cloth and a vial of unknown liquid from an inner pocket. "With a blindfold for your nose."

Truly, the scaleless were weird, but it was good to have interesting friends.

Partner watched the door surrender to Irsh's patient fingers. She was getting better at finding the combinations that caused the ancient magic to surrender. The silence was welcome, if deafening, broken only by the slight hiss of wind passing through the tunnel as the door opened.

Irsh blew out a long breath. "About time."

Partner sat close, absorbing everything he could about the ancient arcana, the *technology*, that he could. His nose blindfold made him feel awkward and silly-looking if he stopped to think about it. He chose to abstain from philosophical concerns. "Problems, Lady Irsh?"

She glanced down. "Wasn't sure I could crack that one."

Partner cocked his head. "It seemed to go quickly."

She nodded. "Yes, but the last several have used the same combination of *buttons*. This one was an older code, what Doyle called the *primary reversion default setting*. Luckily, it worked here."

Partner nodded sagely. "Luckily, we have an expert."

Doyle joined them as the door finished sliding to the left and disappearing into the wall. He whistled. "Isn't that interesting."

Partner looked past the threshold. The room revealed was different that the dragon's tunnels outside. The walls were the silver-white they had been in the first caves, including the floor. Inside, the ancient, magical lights flickered suddenly to life.

Partner started to step forward, diligent in his task as scout, but Irsh held him back. "A few moments, Partner. The air in there is very stale and smells strange."

Partner turned to her with an impish smile, nose still *blindfolded* with the stinky cloth. "All air is currently strange, Irsh."

She laughed quietly. "Okay. More so.

Behind him, Doyle's voice became sharp.

Partner did not recognize any of the astonished profanities, only the tone. "Wizard Doyle?"

He glanced back as the human gulped. "Those are original shipping containers."

Partner understood the context of the words, if not the words themselves. Something brought to this world by the gods when they first fled the motherworld. Unbelievably ancient artifacts, lost and forgotten, locked away in a chamber that could not be opened. One hand strayed to his satchel, psychically touching the great icon inside. He paused to genuflect mentally.

Irsh paused a few more moments, although Partner reflected that her wait was pragmatic, rather than religious. She rose, sniffed carefully, and stepped into the room. The others followed.

Inside, Partner recognized many of the magic runes, what Doyle called *letters*, on the sides of the boxes. He could even recognize some of the words thus formed, having studied them and asking the wizard as they had transcribed the great map from the icon.

He considered the great azure wyrm, apparently asleep in the levels above, as well as the burning remains of his village. "Wizard Doyle, I have a request."

The human looked up from a stack of small cubes tucked into one corner. "Yes, Partner?"

Partner forced the words past a suddenly tense, rebellious jaw. "Which of these will slay a dragon?"

Partner-the adventurer felt his heart race and dread shoot a spurt of hot acid fire into his stomach. Partner-the-dragon-worshiper screamed with dismay in his head. Strong psychic pain wrapped painful hot tentacles around the base of his skull and squeezed, as if punishing his apostasy. Both hands clenched into painful fists. He would have fallen but for Sachesu's mountain-like hand suddenly there to hold him.

The ogre squatted down with concern. "Partner?"

He blinked past the pain. "We were programmed to deify them, Sachesu."

The ogre nodded perceptively. "I understand, my friend. Becoming something greater than the gods intended can be a painful awakening."

Partner nodded silently.

Greater than the gods intended.

Chapter 6: Awakening

A nostril twitched. It was a minor thing, but it heralded wakefulness from slumber.

An eyelid opened next. Just the light-blocking lid, not the flying lid nor the inner-most lid. It cracked halfway, as it to examine the great room.

Nothing was amiss. But still, something had roused him.

The other eye opened. Both came fully open as his dream faded.

Marasem lifted his great azure head from his clawed hands and delicately sniffed the breeze.

Breeze? He was hundreds of feet underground, several awkward turns from sunlight. There should be no breeze.

And yet, there was the faintest one. That was enough to wake him, something new after six hundred and forty three years in this nest. But it did not explain his dismay.

He took a deeper lungful.

There. Human-smell. Ogre-smell.

Invaders.

Someone had snuck into his mountain while he slept. Past his guards, his wyverns, his *machines*. He had been violated. Had the Sky Empire finally decided to renew the war they lost so long ago? Would he need to rouse his brothers? Alert the Empire of the West? Perhaps visit the Great Mother herself?

Such news might improve his breeding stock even more at the next flight.

Marasem sniffed again, tasted these two humans and the ogre that accompanied them.

So. Just scouts, perhaps. At most. More likely thieves. He had many treasures left over from the time when humans alone walked this world. Before *Mustafa* made the lesser bipeds. Before *Ailaendae*, the Great Mother, created wyrmkind. Before history itself.

He turned his great skull and looked back over his right shoulder. There. A ledge overlooking his nest. Had they been spying on him as he slept?

The great wyrm thought back to the founding of his nest. Those tunnels were among the oldest. They had been sealed off from an even-older base when the humans had been driven east-over-mountains. They had somehow found a way through the guardians on the far side and slipped into the back of his fortress.

Who to task? Which of his troglodytes did he trust enough to explore those back chambers, so close to his treasure vaults? None of the wyverns would do. Too much risk of a palace coup. No, he needed one young and ambitious, but not so stupid as to challenge Marasem himself.

Exhane? No, he had already been eaten for his audacity. Had it truly been three decades? Pity. He would have been useful today.

Wuaox, then? Simple, direct, brutal. Tireless. He could chase down a band of thieves and bring them to heel. Yes. It would be nice to hunt men again.

Marasem bellowed for his soldiers as he rose and made his way out of the warm sand pit to the audience chamber where he held court.

Chapter 7: Stealing Fire From The Gods

Doyle rested on his heels and watched. "Okay, repeat it one more time so I am confident you have it down."

Partner tasted the rhythms in his mind, etching them into deepest memory. In his hands, he cradled a short, stout weapon of the ancients. It was his own height, yet remarkably light, made from the magical alloy Doyle called *polymer*. It had a matte black finish, like one of the venomous tunnel vipers that occasionally plagued his village if surprised while hunting rodents.

Partner was sure it had grown warm to his touch, but is he moved a hand, it cooled almost instantly. Partner-the-scholar kept one hand in constant motion as an experiment.

He took a deep breath and began the chant. "This is a fire lance. It contains *ammunition* for three bolts. Each bolt is sufficient to slay any creature up to *Mark 9 face-tempered armour plate*. To arm the lance, the latch is slid open here."

Nimble fingers caressed a pair of buttons, pinched, and pulled them rearward. The lower center of the lance suddenly parted like a fresh chicken egg into two matched halves. Partner eyed the silver and black magical disk at his feet. He lifted it and slid it carefully but forcefully into the gap and felt the lance pull itself closed, as it alive and hungry for murder.

Partner fell into his rhythm again. "Once charged, the weapon seals and arms. The *safety* is right-handed, and located high on the human thumb side when held to fire."

He lifted the artifact and rested it to his shoulder, awkwardly, since his bones were not human, but it was close enough to a fit, according to the wizard. "The fire-lance is brought to the right shoulder, settled firmly against the cheek, and armed. Spot the target through the *heuristic optics* and center the cross, offsetting for *heat-induced shimmer* when engaging at great range."

His thumb found the safety by stretching as far as he could. He moved his hand off the safety, as Doyle had instructed while learning, and mimicked the press down to arm. His hand moved back into position inside the inner ring of the *trigger*, one of the few metal places he could touch. "An Isaurian must use two fingers to pull the trigger, to make up for the lesser travel of the device from safe to fire and smaller hands. The recoil is *backward-vented and minimal*, and the fire-lance returns to the ready position one heartbeat later."

Partner turned to eye the wizard hopefully. "*Ready to disarm?*"

Doyle smiled. "Very well done, Partner. Normally, it would take a *recruit* half a day to learn that ritual. It took you three passes. I'm impressed."

Partner sniffed at his partner. "I am a scholar. We do not have books to remember things for us, so we must remember it for each other."

Sachesu laughed. "You must teach me these tricks, Partner. I was completely lost."

Partner nodded at the ogre, very serious. "Indeed, friend Sachesu. We must make you a scholar as well."

Across the way, Irsh corked her bottle of tea and rose from her seat on the floor. Her backpack was crammed with one of the smaller boxes. "Doyle, do we really have to leave most of this here?"

The wizard nodded. "Unfortunately, yes. While we could empty the boxes of the treasure, having the treasure containers makes them worth several times as much. What I plan to do is get back to town and arrange for us to have a couple of wagons, teamsters, and some sledges we can haul down here to properly loot the place. You have no idea what I could sell this stuff for, back home."

Partner's ear stubs perked up. "Where is home, friend Doyle? I have met many species on my adventure, but I have never seen a human with skin so dark brown as yours. Most humans, such as Irsh, are so pale as to be a faded pink."

He watched the human struggle with an answer. "I was born in a city known as Ithome in what you would call the kingdom of Ballard. It is so very far away from here, into the rising sun, that you would not comprehend the distances involved."

Sachesu's face grew serious. "East across the sea?"

Doyle nodded. "As good a term as any."

Irsh pointed. "So why does he get to take a firelance himself?"

Doyle started to reply, but Partner cut him off. "Because the map that led us here belonged to my village, before the wyverns destroyed my kin. The fire lance is my price for the rest."

Irsh's eyes blinked in a human version of surprise. Even Partner-the-scholar quailed a little at the fierce determination in his voice. Eldest Brother would be absolutely aghast at what he had turned into. But, hopefully, proud.

The War For Eternity was about to begin, led by the smallest Isaurian.

Chapter 8: Escape

Partner looked up interested as Sachesu shaded his eyes to get a better view. "Doyle, can I borrow your far-seeing artifact? We might have company."

Heads instantly rotated to the south. Doyle reached into his over-stuffed backpack and pulled out a small rounded box, made of the magical *polymer*, with a place for eyes to rest on one side and a large glass lens on the other. He handed it wordlessly to the ogre and helped Irsh the rest of the way out of the pit.

Sachesu studied the distant hillside and whistled. "Yes, they've definitely seen us and are coming this way."

Irsh let go of the rope as she made it to solid ground. "Can we outrun them?"

The giant handed the magic lenses back to Doyle. "Maybe. They appear to be on foot, so an infantry column."

Doyle stuffed the *binoculars* away and started moving north. "If we can get to cover, we can try to lose them in the trees.

Sachesu nodded. "Agreed. Partner, would it be acceptable if I carried you for the first distance?"

Partner grabbed his satchel tightly and relaxed as he stepped into the ogre's grip. The fire lance strapped across his back made his balance feel strange. "Certainly, friend. Let us escape."

Sachesu set off at a soft jog, his long legs forcing Irsh and Doyle to almost run to keep up. "Partner, how fast can troglodytes move?"

Partner considered the many factors involved. He had never worked with humans before, so he only had stories and legends as he contemplated the dark line on the distant hillside pointed this way. "Over a short distance, I believe they can run faster, Sachesu, but it is an explosive movement that cannot be sustained over any great period. We should be able to make it to the trees well ahead of them and then hopefully disappear."

The trio set off at a ground-eating jog, glancing back occasionally. The column of troops continued to point right at them like an arrow of doom.

～

Partner heard a sound above the pounding of feet and looked to the sky. He felt his mind go, again, as the iridescent blue scales caught the afternoon light.

Partner-the-dragon-worshiper sighed happily inside. Partner-the-scholar studied the complex interplay of muscles and physics and marveled that the creature swooping in from behind had been designed and built from human stock originally, as had all intelligent creatures in the world. Partner-the-adventurer cried out, but he was pushed into a quiet corner by the dragon-worshiper and left silent and impotent.

Partner-the-adventurer pushed hard against the chains binding his mind. He railed. He raged. He kicked and bit and clawed. He howled profanities he had learned from Doyle, and Irsh, and even the great ogre philosopher, Sachesu.

A whisper escaped his constricted throat. "Dragon."

Sachesu glanced down as he loped along. "What was that, Partner?"

The ogre's words created an opening in the sheet of glass separating Partner from the outside world. In his mind, he stuck a finger into that hole and pulled, stretching it wider and tearing with all his might as he fought to pull himself through it and escape the trap built there by the Great Mother.

He took a breath across a suddenly dry mouth. He swallowed hard. The words came out almost audible. "Dragon."

Irsh jogged alongside. "Did he say dragon?"

Partner screamed one last time in his mind. The chains shattered, freeing him, but he was too late. The great wyrm was just above them, swooping in hard, mouth agape, feet tucked back. Partner saw the chest swell. "Dragon!"

Heads turned. Gasps.

And then the dragon breathed and a cloud of icy death engulfed them.

Partner staggered back to consciousness across a field of sharp lava crystals in his mind, bleeding and forlorn, limbs bound and rigid. He forced open his eyes.

A shadow raced across the ground in front of him, dragon shaped. Troglodytes loped the last hundred yards. Irsh lay a few yards away, eyes closed and unconscious, but apparently still breathing. Doyle appeared a few feet beyond.

Cold invaded his consciousness as he woke up and felt the stun ebb away. A great weight pressed him to the ground. Partner turned his head.

Sachesu had apparently sheltered him from the dragon's breath at the last moment. Partner was cradled against the ogre's chest, underneath him, safe. Partner reached out a hand and found several inches of ice forming a solid shield across the ogre's back.

Partner looked again at the ground and saw a field of ice in the space between he and Irsh.

The great ogre philosopher had protected him from the blast when it came.

Partner reached out and closed the ogre's eyes, once bright green, now faded in death.

Slowly, awkwardly, Partner pulled himself from under the tremendous weight of his friend and stood, careful on the sheet of new ice.

He looked down and saw Doyle blink, but saw no mind behind the eyes.

So, he was alone, facing his worst enemies, his greatest nightmare.

The great blue wyrm circled one last time and them glided in to land, as graceful as a raptor coming to roost. Two great, horn-protected eyes focused on him with keen interest.

Partner-the-dragon-worshipper fell to his knees in awe and fervor, taking the body with him. Partner-the-scholar gibbered in terror. Partner-the-adventurer glanced down at his fallen friends and whimpered.

The wyrm spoke in the vast hollow emptiness, a surprisingly rich tenor for such a deep chest. "Wuaox, bring the Isaurian thief when you kill the others. I want to know what secrets they learned."

Partner watched a troglodyte in a complicated uniform salute, sword in hand more as a swagger stick than a threat. Here was the least of the lizardkind, confronted by one of his gods. What threat could such a little creature present?

Partner-the-scholar absently cataloged the approaching troops. Troglodytes all, in good order. No wyverns were present. The great god sat on a rise and surveyed his kingdom, as was his right.

The captain, Wuaox, walked closer, sneered "We're not going to have any trouble with you, are we, thief?"

Partner-the-dragon-worshipper quietly whispered. "No, master."

Master. Master?

Partner-the-dragon-worshipper happily submitted. Partner-the-scholar itemized his sins. Partner-the-adventurer looked forward to a rough and painful death in failure.

Master?

And then a new voice entered his mind. Partner had forgotten the voice, suppressed in the grand adventure of becoming something so much greater than the gods had intended. Youngest Brother looked down at his fallen friend and contemplated a world that would never know an ogre philosopher.

In his mind, Youngest Brother screamed pure rage.

Almost faster than the eye could follow, a hand slipped under his cape and drew forth the fire lance. He had never unloaded it after the last lesson.

Perhaps, he had known it would be thus.

Youngest Brother flipped the artifact to his shoulder as his thumb found the safety and flipped it off for the first time in several millennia.

Two sturdy fingers caressed the trigger as he crossed a dragon's surprised face and a songbird suddenly awoke in his ear.

Youngest Brother screamed, aloud this time, as he stroked the trigger from rest to death.

A lightning bolt erupted from his hands, connecting his life with the great wyrm who would be his god. The intense blue light was almost too much to live through. He wanted to cease, rather than live with the shame of having watched his friend die.

Downrange, the lightning bolt liberated all of its terrible energy on the form of a great blue dragon known as Marasem.

The god fell to the ground in pieces.

A troglodyte spoke. "What?"

In his mind, Youngest Brother heard Eldest Brother scream in agony as their village burned. He turned the fire lance on the lizardman captain and pulled the trigger a second time. The troglodyte simply exploded, like a star brought to earth.

Youngest Brother took a stride forward towards the assembled troops, suddenly cowering in astonished fear.

His rage had slain a god.

He became Death itself and howled at them.

"Run!"

Like spooked antelope, they scattered, tripping over each other and trampling the fallen underfoot.

In moments, Partner-the-dragon-slayer held the field, alone.

Youngest Brother cried.

⚊

Silence.

Behind him, a voice stirred. Doyle's mind had finally returned. "Partner?"

Partner turned and walked to where the wizard sat.

Doyle rubbed his eyes and flexed his hands to restore circulation. "What happened?"

Partner saw Irsh begin to stir as well. He walked over and helped lift her to a seated position. He pulled her warm tea flask from her backpack and opened it, watched her greedily suck down the heat like a newborn kit.

Partner looked one last time before he turned back to the human wizard. "Sachesu is dead."

Doyle's mind finally registered the giant blue shape piled nearby. "What is that?"

Youngest Brother sighed. "And I have slain a god."

Chapter 9: *The Last Waltz*

Partner pulled the trigger on the fire lance, watched the mountainside hump up suddenly under the caress of blue lightning and then collapse over the cave where they had lain Sachesu's body. Moments later, a very polite, almost diffident, avalanche subsided, burying the ogre under half a mountain.

Partner chanted the ritual under his breath as he opened the fire lance and removed the spent *ammunition magazine* reverently. It was still warm to the touch as he wrapped it in a cloth and placed it in his satchel next to the great icon, the *nav beacon*, that thing that had made the quest possible. That *ammunition magazine* would form part of the legend he would take with him when he told the tales of the great ogre philosopher who had been his friend.

He felt Irsh put a warm, comforting hand on his shoulder as he sighed. He glanced up, saw the pained smile on her face. He nodded and placed his hand over hers. Truly, friends he could have never imagined when it all began.

They turned as Doyle's voice broke the silence. "Affirmative, Stig. I see your landing glare. Put her down on the flat below us where I left the signal. We'll come down when it cools."

Partner understood every word spoken by the wizard. He had no idea what the man had just said. Instead, he turned to the east and watched a star detach itself from the morning sun, accompanied by a pulsing rumble louder and steadier than the landslide had been.

Over the rising thunder, Partner called out. "Friend Doyle, what is that?"

The wizard turned and fixed him with a deadly serious look. "That is my ship. That is *Ngoma Mwisho. The Last Waltz.*

Irsh's voice broke midway through her words. "But it's flying."

The human nodded.

Partner stepped closer as the din escalated. "Are you a god?"

The wizard shook his head. "No, Partner. I am merely a wizard. Come. There are some people I want you to meet."

Partner marveled at the great ship as it rested on the rock. Up close, it looked like a sleek, metallic beast of prey, somewhere between gray and silver in color. Doyle had called it a hammerhead shark, but Partner had never seen such a creature, so he could only guess at the comparison. He could tell that it was huge, hundreds of paces long. And that it had flown here and landed on fire. The rocks had only now cooled enough to be uncomfortable instead of lethal.

From the bow end of the shark, where Doyle had said a hammerhead would have an eye, a doorway irised open. So, eye-like. Human eyes.

A ramp slid out like a great metal tongue.

At the top, movement.

A female emerged, began to walk down the ramp. Her clothing left no doubt as to her gender, but Partner had never seen anything like the materials from which it was made. But it was the woman herself that drew his eye, and then his mind.

Like Doyle she had skin that same dark, creamy brown, and the same deep brown hair in tight curls, but cut so close on the sides he could see her skin. In her hands, she carried some strange artifact made of the magical *polymer*. From her manner, it was a weapon. She did not, quite, point it at him.

The wizard strode forward. He said something in a language Partner had never encountered before, filled with rich vowels. The woman looked closely at the wizard, and then slid the weapon into a belt pouch that hung to her thigh.

They exchanged a hug that was less than lovers and more than companions. Doyle kissed her on a cheek. He smiled and turned to face them, one hand lightly around her back, hip to hip on the side without the weapon.

Doyle gestured as he spoke. "Piper, these are my companions, Irsh and Partner."

Partner watched her mannerisms closely, learning a whole new human body language as she smiled and spoke. *"Ni vizuri kukutana na wewe."*

Doyle translated with warmth. "She said she is pleased to meet you. Irsh, Partner, this is my niece, Piper Iwakuma-Holmström."

Irsh was silent, still shocked by the turn of events. Partner spoke up in her stead. "And we are very pleased to meet you, Friend Piper."

Piper blinked at him in surprise, and then smiled warmly. With her free hand, she pointed back over her left, disbelief evident in her tones. *"Ni kwamba joka?"*

Doyle laughed affectionately. "Indeed it is. My little friend here, Partner, killed a god."

~~

The collected group sat around a fire built up of brush as the sun set, and consumed the most interesting meal Partner could have ever imagined, steaks carved from the ribs of a fallen god.

In addition to Piper, Partner had met the other two members of Doyle's crew, a towering blond human named Bjorn who was Piper's mate, and a second cousin, Stig Tjäder, who was an average-sized human with hair almost the same blood red shade as Irsh's, and a booming laugh. He sat close to Irsh and engaged in preliminary mating rituals, possibly with some success, although human interactions were still a new language for Partner.

Partner considered his friends as he chewed. The meat was tender and wonderful in his mouth, for all it left behind the taste of ashes. He missed Sachesu. He missed his friend.

Partner interrupted Doyle's stream of translation between players to ask a simple question. "Doyle, if you had this ship, this power, why all the secrecy? You could have taken anything you wanted from the troglodytes."

The murmurs died down. Doyle took a drink from a glass bottle that smelled of fermented fruit juice and settled himself. "Because it would never have helped your world."

Partner cocked his head to the side as he had learned from his friends.

Doyle grinned wryly at him. "If I did that, it would be just another war among the gods. But you, my friend, you have done something that nobody has ever done. You have slain a dragon, a god, if you will. The whole world will tremble."

He paused to repeat the words for his kin-group. They nodded and murmured.

Doyle took another sip. "And you will have tokens of that feat. And stories and witnesses. But it is necessary to move very fast right now, to exploit the situation."

He translated again, and then paused to listen to a question from Piper. "Ndiyo, Piper. Yes."

Doyle's arms expanded to encompass the group, and the whole world. "Another dragon will come, and take charge, but not before we can sneak in the back way with a few *hoversleds*, and steal all the dragon's treasure. And bring with us enough arcane *firepower* to destroy any troglodytes that wish to gainsay us."

Partner nodded. "And what will you do with the treasure, Doyle?"

The wizard paused. Partner had become adept at reading his face. Several answers were considered and discarded. "Partner, all the worlds of the Confederation fell into barbarism when the Cataclysm came. Many of them simply died. A few, like Ballard, my home, survived, but even today we cannot reproduce the artifacts of the ancients, the *technology*. That treasure will make me rich beyond any measure on this world, but it will also help all of humanity recover some of what was lost."

The wizard paused to let that sink in.

He finished his bottle and carefully opened a second one, identical. "And I promised a great reward. Irsh, I can give you wealth to make your wildest dreams come true. What do you desire?"

Partner watched the woman weigh her options. She smiled hesitantly at Stig. He returned it, just as hesitantly. She looked around the group slowly, and then glanced at the shattered hillside in the distance. "I think I would like to see what is beyond the sky."

Partner watched the wizard and his niece negotiate with eyebrow movements and nods and shakes. The outcome seemed good. "That is within my power to grant, Irshandra, daughter of Ayya. I will work you like a beast of the field, and Bjorn will teach you how to be a spacer. But the things you will see."

Doyle turned to him. "And you, Partner? Half of all this is yours. Do you wish to see the stars?"

Youngest Brother considered the crew of the strange ship, of *The Last Waltz*. He watched Irsh tentatively hold hands with Stig. He looked up at the tomb of his friend. He turned his eyes toward the wizard Doyle. The stranger who came from beyond the sky. He nodded and smiled sadly.

"It is necessary that I remain in this place, Doyle. I have a story to tell, about a great ogre philosopher, and world that needs to hear it..."

About the Author

Blaze has lived in many different places, including Kansas, The Ozarks, Breckenridge, and SoCal. He's also done a number of things, some of which are even past the statute of limitations now. The ones he'll tell you about (without the need for full anonymity) include being a bouncer at a cowboy bar outside a Marine base, a volunteer storm-spotter with the county fire department, and herding nerds at a small software company. He currently lives Seattle-ish and tells stories in most every form of English you can, and a few other languages.

About Knotted Road Press

Knotted Road Press fiction specializes in dynamic writing set in mysterious, exotic locations.

Knotted Road Press non-fiction publishes autobiographies, cookbooks, and how-to books with unique voices.

Knotted Road Press creates DRM-free ebooks as well as high-quality print books for readers around the world.

With authors in a variety of genres including literary, poetry, mystery, fantasy, and science fiction, Knotted Road Press has something for everyone.

Knotted Road Press
www.KnottedRoadPress.com

Also available from Knotted Road Press

Beyond the Mirror: Volume 1 Fantastic Worlds

Find it online at www.KnottedRoadPress.com or at your favorite bookseller